*The
United States
in
World War
I*

THE UNITED STATES
IN WORLD WAR I

*Illustrated
with
photographs,
and maps
by
Robert Standley*

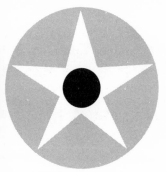

DON LAWSON

*The Story
of General
John J. Pershing
and the
American
Expeditionary
Forces*

*Abelard-Schuman
New York*

BOOKS BY DON LAWSON

The Young People's History of America's Wars Series

The Colonial Wars: *Prelude to the American Revolution*
(ISBN: 0-200-71885-1)

The American Revolution: *America's First War for Independence*
(ISBN: 0-200-00131-0)

The War of 1812: *America's Second War for Independence*
(ISBN: 0-200-71441-4)

The United States in the Indian Wars
(ISBN: 0-200-00158-2)

The United States in the Spanish-American War
(ISBN: 0-200-00163-9)

The United States in World War I: *The Story of General
John J. Pershing and the American Expeditionary Forces*
(ISBN: 0-200-71939-4)

The United States in World War II: *Crusade for World Freedom*
(ISBN: 0-200-71795-2)

The United States in the Korean War:
Defending Freedom's Frontier
(ISBN: 0-200-71803-7)

© *Copyright 1963 by Don Lawson*
L. C. Card Number: 63-8233
Published in Canada by Fitzhenry & Whiteside Limited, Toronto.

Printed in the United States of America
Designed by The Etheredges

ISBN 0-200-71939-4

4   5   6   7   8   9   10

To
the memory of
my uncle,
Bert Furguson,
whose
stories about the
A.E.F.
were such an
important
part of
my boyhood

Acknowledgments

Librarians are, of course, extremely important to readers, but to writers they are absolutely indispensable. This writer is eternally in their debt. I should like particularly to thank Helen C. Bough, Supervisor of Work with Children, Chicago Public Library, who suggested that this book be written; Wayne M. Hartwell, Editorial Librarian, F. E. Compton & Co., who aided me in research and in preparing the bibliography; Margaret Scriven, Librarian, Chicago Historical Society, who made available to me the files of the Chicago *Tribune* and other daily newspapers covering the period of World War I; and Wyllis E. Wright, Librarian, Williams College Library, who generously provided me with a photostatic copy of the German surrender demand to Major Charles Whittlesey of the Lost Battalion.

I also wish particularly to thank Captain Eddie Rickenbacker for permission to use the lines from his war diary

9

as well as for his generosity in taking time from his busy schedule as an airlines executive to answer my inquiries. Tony March, Editor, Army *Times,* was a great aid in tracking down obscure news clips on the Lost Battalion and the Unknown Soldier. Grant Nash, Rainbow Division veteran, was most helpful in supplying me with combat information in general and details about Big Bertha in particular.

The Smithsonian Institution, the National Archives, and the United States Army and United States Air Force offices of information were especially generous in providing me with photographs.

I also wish to thank Verne Pore for preparing the index, and Eleanor Brooks for typing the final manuscript.

Finally I am most grateful to my good wife, Beatrice, for her assistance and encouragement above and beyond the call of duty.

Acknowledgment is gratefully made to the following publishers for permission to use excerpts from books on their lists:

G. P. Putnam's Sons: *Five Down and Glory* by Gene Gurney, copyright 1958.

J. B. Lippincott Company: *My Experiences in the World War* by John J. Pershing; and *Fighting the Flying Circus* by Edward V. Rickenbacker.

—DON LAWSON

Contents

Illustrations

13

Foreword

This book tells the story of the American Expeditionary Forces in World War I. It is important for the reader to remember that the other Allies had been engaged in this conflict for more than two-and-a-half years before America's entry.

Each life is a small miracle. Thus it is not wholly fitting to say that one nation lost "only" so many men as compared with another nation's far greater losses. Nevertheless it is true that the United States had about 50,000 men killed, while Great Britain and France, for example, counted their dead in the millions.

Most historians agree, however, that the A.E.F. turned the tide of battle from stalemate and possible defeat into Allied victory on the Western Front.

15

*The
United States
in
World War
I*

"Lafayette,
We
Are Here!"

It was a bright spring day in the year 1917. A ramrod-straight, granite-jawed United States Regular Army officer stood before the desk of the Secretary of War, Newton D. Baker, in Washington, D. C.

"How well do you write and speak French?" Secretary Baker asked.

The officer hesitated only a moment. "Fairly well, sir. A few years ago I spent several months in France learning the language. I could relearn it quickly."

The slight, rather prim little man behind the desk carefully studied the officer before him. "Good," he said finally. "President Wilson and I want you to take command of the American Expeditionary Forces. How soon can you assemble a staff and get to France?"

General John J. Pershing was surprised, in fact startled by Secretary Baker's words, but his face did not show it. Only his jaw muscles tightened and the firm line of his chin seemed to grow even firmer. He had come to Washington expecting to be put in charge of a military division. He had never even considered the possibility of his being made Commanding General of the A.E.F. But he was somewhat accustomed to such surprises, and he was more than accustomed to assuming command. Now he thought about Secretary Baker's words. How soon could he get to France? This was the middle of May. The United States had been at war with Germany since early in April.

"I can be in France by the end of next month," General Pershing said.

As Pershing left the Secretary of War's office he was smiling to himself. He was thinking of the time not too long ago when he had seriously considered quitting the Army because he was not being promoted fast enough. Then President Theodore Roosevelt had promoted him from captain to brigadier general over the heads of 862 officers who outranked him.

Suddenly the smile left Pershing's face as he thought of his wife, Frances. This would have been a proud day for her—for her and their three little girls who were no longer living. Forcing the thought from his mind, General Pershing squared his shoulders. There was work to be done.

Pershing was now 57, but he was as eager to succeed in this new job as he had been when he had started teaching school back in his home state of Missouri at the age of 17. Later he had attended a teachers' training school at Kirksville, Missouri. One day while he was in college he saw an announcement that competitive examinations were

General John J. Pershing, Commander-in-Chief of the American Expeditionary Forces. (U.S. Army photograph).

being held for entrance into West Point. He certainly had no intention of becoming a soldier, but he did want a free education. He took the examination and won the appointment by a single grade point.

After his graduation from West Point in 1886 he had served at a number of Army posts. It had been a hard and lonely life, but it had taught him a great deal about self-discipline and how to lead other men. It had also been a dangerous life, particularly when he had taken part in the fighting against the savage Apache and Sioux Indians. Later he was made an instructor of military tactics at the University of Nebraska and at West Point. While teaching at Nebraska he also studied law and received his law degree. Ever since then he had been looking forward to the day when he could retire from the Army and take up the private practice of law. But he always felt his duty to his country as a soldier came first.

When the Spanish-American war began in 1898 Pershing returned to active military service and fought in the battle of San Juan Hill as a lieutenant in the cavalry. His commanding officer described him as "the coolest man under fire I have ever seen." When the war ended Pershing was sent to the Philippine Islands where he helped subdue the savage tribes of Moros. His successful work there resulted in his appointment to the General Staff Corps back in the United States.

In 1905 Pershing married Frances Warren, the daughter of Senator Francis Warren, and the lovely young bride seemed to bring new meaning to the lonely soldier's life. They had four children, a son and three daughters, who meant more to Pershing than all of the medals that had ever been struck. Then, while he was serving at the

Presidio, an Army post in San Francisco, stark tragedy entered his life. On August 27, 1912, Pershing was on duty away from the Presidio when a fire raged through the post, killing his wife and three daughters. Only his son, Warren, was saved.

Pershing buried his grief beneath a mountain of Army staff work. Except for his son, this was the only love he now had. In the end, however, he and the Army were to serve each other well.

General Pershing had been brought to the attention of Newton Baker shortly after Baker entered President Woodrow Wilson's cabinet as Secretary of War. On March 8, 1916, a Mexican bandit chief, Francisco "Pancho" Villa, and his men raided the town of Columbus, New Mexico. They had burned the town and killed 16 United States citizens. Baker's first official act had been to sign the orders sending an expedition of United States Army troops into Mexico to capture Villa and his henchmen. Pershing had been placed in command of this expedition.

Although Villa had not been caught, his gang of bandits had been scattered and their leader wounded. Villa himself undoubtedly could have been captured if Pershing had been allowed to pursue him farther. The Mexican government, however, had insisted that all American troops be removed from Mexico. In fact, there was even a threat of full-scale war with Mexico if they were not removed.

In the face of such threats, both Baker and President Wilson agreed that Pershing had handled himself and his troops very well. They also agreed that Pershing seemed suited for an important American role in the war that was raging in Europe. The job as Commanding General of the

American Expeditionary Forces had been the result.

*   *   *

General Pershing and his staff arrived in France on June 13, 1917. Two weeks later the people of St. Nazaire watched the first convoy of ships carrying American troops steam into the harbor. On July 4, America's Independence Day, a battalion of United States Regular Army men of the 1st Division paraded through the streets of Paris. They were then led by General Pershing to the tomb of the Marquis de Lafayette, the French nobleman who had played such a heroic role in helping the United States win the Revolutionary War. Now the United States, with the first American army ever sent to Europe, was preparing to repay that debt.

Not only the French but people throughout the Allied world were thrilled when their newspapers reported that as he stood by Lafayette's tomb, General Pershing said:

"Lafayette, we are here!"

Afterwards General Pershing insisted that not he but one of his aides, Colonel Charles E. Stanton, had actually spoken the ringing phrase. Nevertheless it was credited to Pershing, and the words were electric with promise and bright hope at a time when the Allied cause looked as dark as it had at any time since the start of World War I in 1914.

Two

*The
War Before
America's
Entry*

A young man by the name of Gavrilo Princip had committed the specific act that started the war. It was he who assassinated Archduke Francis Ferdinand, heir to the throne of Austria-Hungary, and the Archduke's wife, Sophie. The incident took place during a parade at Sarajevo in Bosnia on June 28, 1914. War had been threatening Europe for more than a decade. Young Princip's murderous deed in the Balkans was the spark that set the smoldering nations aflame.

Princip belonged to a patriotic group of young Serbian students who had been fighting to unite all of their people and free them from Austrian rule. Austria-Hungary now said that Serbia was responsible for the assassination. A 48-hour ultimatum was delivered to Serbia. In this action

Austria was firmly backed by its ally, Germany, and by the German Emperor, Kaiser Wilhelm (William II). Serbia avoided a direct reply and began to mobilize its army. On July 28 Austria-Hungary declared war on its small neighbor.

Rival European nations had been engaged in an arms race for many years. They had also been busy making protective alliances among one another. In a sense these alliances were designed to prevent a general war. They were so set up, however, that an attack by one nation upon another was almost certain to trigger just such a war.

When Austria presented its harsh ultimatum to Serbia, Russia also mobilized its troops. The Russians had their own plans for Balkan rule. They also wanted to conquer Turkey and gain control of the straits of the Dardanelles. Germany gave Russia just 12 hours to call off its mobilization. Russia refused. Germany then declared war not only on Russia but also on France, since the Germans knew France was pledged to fight if Russia were attacked. France had been wanting revenge for its defeat in the Franco-Prussian War of 1870-71. The French welcomed this opportunity not only to avenge that defeat but also to regain their lost provinces of Alsace and Lorraine.

Great Britain had a so-called "cordial understanding" with France. This meant that England would go to war if France were attacked. In addition, England and Germany had been rival sea powers for many years. This rivalry had begun in the 1890's when Kaiser Wilhelm spurred Germany into building a fleet as large as England's. England met the challenge then, and it was prepared to meet the Kaiser's challenge now with a declaration of war if necessary.

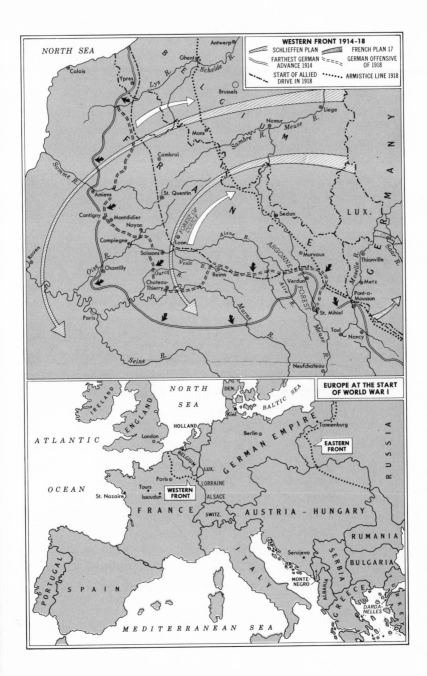

WESTERN FRONT 1914-18

SCHLIEFFEN PLAN
FARTHEST GERMAN ADVANCE 1914
START OF ALLIED DRIVE IN 1918
FRENCH PLAN 17
GERMAN OFFENSIVE OF 1918
ARMISTICE LINE 1918

NORTH SEA

Calais
Ypres
Ghents
Antwerp
Brussels
Schelde R.
Lys R.
Liege
Namur
Meuse R.
Mons
Sambre R.
Cambrai
Somme R.
Amiens
St. Quentin
Cantigny
Montdidier
Noyon
Compiegne
Soissons
FOREST OF COUCY
Laon
Aisne R.
Sedan
LUX.
Murvaux
Thionville
Metz
Rouen
Oise R.
Chantilly
Ourcq
Vesle R.
Reims
ARGONNE FOREST
Verdun
Aire R.
Pont-a-Mousson
Chateau-Thierry
Paris
Marne R.
St. Mihiel
Toul
Nancy
Seine R.
Meuse R.
Neufchateau
GERMANY

EUROPE AT THE START OF WORLD WAR I

ATLANTIC
OCEAN
IRELAND
ENGLAND
London
NORTH SEA
DEN.
Kiel
BALTIC SEA
HOLLAND
BELGIUM
LUX.
Paris
LORRAINE
ALSACE
Tours
Issoudun
St. Nazaire
FRANCE
SWITZ.
GERMAN EMPIRE
Berlin
Tannenburg
EASTERN FRONT
RUSSIA
WESTERN FRONT
AUSTRIA - HUNGARY
RUMANIA
ITALY
Serajevo
SERBIA
BULGARIA
MONTE-NEGRO
ALBANIA
GREECE
TURKEY
DARDA-NELLES
PORTUGAL
SPAIN
MEDITERRANEAN SEA

The immediate cause for Great Britain's declaration of war, however, was Germany's attack on Belgium, whose neutrality all of the nations were pledged to respect. Germany violated this pledge by crossing the neutral nation's borders in early August. When England demanded that the German troops be removed, the German Chancellor, Theobold von Bethmann-Hollweg, said, "England is going to declare war against us over a scrap of paper." The "scrap of paper" was England's guarantee of Belgium's neutrality. England honored it with a declaration of war on August 4. This brought the British Empire into the conflict.

As the war went on, many other nations took part. Turkey and Bulgaria sided with Germany and Austria-Hungary. These nations were called the Central Powers. Among the countries that later took part actively on the side of the Allies were Italy, Japan, Greece, Montenegro, Portugal, Rumania, and the United States.

*   *   *

When the war began all of the nations involved thought it would end quickly. Both Germany and France had master plans for swiftly defeating one another. Germany's Schlieffen plan was named after General Alfred von Schlieffen, who died in 1913 shortly before the war began.

The Schlieffen plan was somewhat like the tactics a boxer uses as he jabs with his left hand to keep an opponent off balance and then throws a long, looping right-hand punch directly to his opponent's jaw. The "left jab" in this case was to be a small number of German defensive troops on the left flank to hold the attacking French at the Rhine River. The great bulk of Germany's troops were to be used on the right flank. They would swing down through Belgium and northern France like a right-hand punch aimed at knocking out Paris, the French capital.

Schlieffen felt that his plan would be successful only if it were followed to the letter. On his death bed he was reported to have said, "It must come to a fight. Only remember to make the right flank strong."

When World War I actually started, the Schlieffen plan was changed by events and by General Helmuth von Moltke. First of all, more troops than Schlieffen had anticipated had to be used on the Eastern Front to hold Russia at bay. Secondly, von Moltke weakened the plan by trying to strengthen *both* the left and right flanks in the attack against France. There were simply not enough German combat troops available to make all of this possible. Finally, the French had their own plan of attack on Germany. It was called Plan 17, and included a powerful blow to be aimed at the German center and left at the city of Metz and the provinces of Alsace and Lorraine.

In the first weeks of the war Germany's Schlieffen plan almost succeeded. The long, looping right hand that was the German army's right flank struck successfully through Belgium and on down into France. Heroic but futile efforts to parry the blow were made by the Belgians at Liége, the British at Mons, and the French at Charleroi.

By early September the Germans were 15 miles from Paris. At this point, on September 6, French General Joseph Joffre issued an order to his troops "to die where you stand rather than give way." Reserve troops were rushed from the capital in every available vehicle, including buses and taxicabs. The British army, under Sir John French, attacked the onrushing Germans on one flank, while the famed French "taxicab army" attacked them on the other flank. The Germans' knockout blow failed to strike Paris. Within four days the Germans were driven back to the Aisne River, ending the epic First Battle of the Marne.

Shortly before the Battle of the Marne a German general had sent a telegraph message to Berlin saying, "Victory is ours!" Now the Germans had suffered their first defeat. They also had to worry about fighting a war not only on the Western Front but also on the Eastern Front against Russia. The Schlieffen plan had been designed to prevent this with a quick defeat of France.

The French found that their Plan 17 had also failed them. A key part of Plan 17 had been the idea that no matter what happened the French would be always on the offensive. "Attack! Attack!" had been the slogan in all of the military training classes. There had been little chance, however, to put the slogan to work in the face of the onrushing German armies until the stand before Paris.

The British were also licking their wounds and realizing that the war that was predicted to end in a few weeks or months might go on for at least one more year. The only person who would dare voice the thought that the fighting might continue even longer, perhaps for years, was Britain's Sir Douglas Haig. Nobody would believe him.

By the end of 1914, the war on the Western Front had settled into a stalemate. Both sides held lines of trenches that extended from Switzerland to the English Channel. These trenches were actually fortresses in which the soldiers hid to protect themselves from rifle and machine-gun fire and artillery bombardment. The dream of a dashing war of attack was thus turned into a nightmare of siege warfare that had not been seen in Europe since the 18th century. Even one of the weapons for attacking these trenches was one used by 18th-century grenadiers. This was the hand grenade.

There were, however, a number of new methods that were either developed or perfected for waging war on land, at sea, and in the air in World War I. The machine gun and rapid-fire artillery were among the most important. They were mainly responsible for turning a war of movement into one of siege. The wireless telegraph speeded communications, and automobiles and trucks speeded transportation.

The Germans first used poisonous gas in an attack on the Russians in the Masurian Lakes region on January 31, 1915. The first effective use of poisonous gas, however, was by the Germans in an attack against the French at Ypres on April 22, 1915. Thereafter, gas was used by both sides. The Germans also developed the flame thrower (*flammenwerfer*). The British developed the tank, adapting the idea from the American farm tractor. It was called a tank because—to keep the invention secret—the British workmen who made the first models were told they were making gasoline containers or fuel tanks.

The use of the submarine as an offensive war weapon dated all the way back to the American Revolutionary War. In 1776 the *Turtle,* invented by David Bushnell, made an unsuccessful attempt to sink a British man-of-war, H.M.S. *Eagle,* in New York harbor. In 1864, during the American Civil War, a Confederate submarine, the *Hunley,* sank a Federal ship, the *Housatonic,* in Charleston harbor. This was the first recorded sinking of a warship by a submarine. It was not until World War I, however, that the submarine was used effectively as a war weapon.

Balloons had been used for observation in the American Civil War, and they continued to be used for that purpose by both sides in World War I. Another kind of balloon, however, was developed for war by the Germans. This was the Zeppelin, a rigid-bodied, motor-powered, lighter-than-air craft. It was developed by Count Ferdinand von Zeppelin, who had served as a volunteer with the Federal army during the American Civil War. After his first ride in an observation balloon he began to make plans for his rigid aircraft. Zeppelins first dropped bombs on Paris and London in 1915.

The airplane was also used as an important war weapon for the first time in World War I, both by the Allies and Central Powers. At first airplanes, like balloons, were used, only for observation. Then some unknown pilot decided to throw a hand grenade at a passing enemy plane. Soon pilots on both sides were taking aloft grenades, revolvers, and rifles, and attacking one another. Thus the war in the air began. The first aerial victory may have been won by British pilot Vessy Holt, who fired his revolver at a passing German observation plane and forced it to land behind the Allied lines. This was in 1915.

Also in 1915 a French pilot named Roland Garros successfully experimented with firing a mounted machine gun through the propeller of his plane. Garros put metal strips on the blades of the propeller so that any bullets that hit the blades would bounce off. With this primitive device he quickly shot down five German planes, and the French began calling him the "Ace of all flyers." Soon it became the custom to call every flyer who shot down five planes an Ace.

Garros was later shot down by the Germans and the principle of his device was copied and perfected by a Dutch inventor, Anthony Fokker. Fokker's improvement was a gear that kept the machine gun from firing when the propeller blades were in front of the gun barrel. Thus no bullets could hit the propeller. This so-called "interruptor gear" revolutionized aerial warfare and for a time gave Germany command of the air. The balance was restored when a Rumanian inventor, George Constancesco, developed a hydraulic synchronization system for the British.

*   *   *

During 1915 the stalemate continued on the Western Front. Both the British and French made costly and unsuccessful attacks in Flanders and Champagne. The Germans went on the defensive in the west, turning to Russia on the Eastern Front. The Russians had been badly defeated by the Germans under General Paul von Hindenburg at Tannenberg in 1914. This victory made Hindenburg a national hero in Germany. He and General Erich Ludendorff led the German armies to new victories against the Russians in 1915. In 1916, however, the Russians attacked successfully on the Austrian front, but once again they had so many casualties that they were all but knocked out of the war.

On the Western Front in February 1916, the Germans began an attack on the fortresses at Verdun that lasted for several months. Here was born the famed French battle cry that became the slogan for all of the Allies: "They shall not pass!" The stirring phrase was credited to General Henri Pétain, but it actually appeared in an order issued by Pétain's successor at Verdun, General Robert Nivelle.

When the Germans finally failed to take Verdun, the French counterattacked for several more months in the same area. Also during 1916 the British attacked in the Somme area but failed to gain a decisive victory. It was here, on September 15, that tanks were first used in combat. Although their first use by the British was not particularly successful, tanks were soon being manufactured by all of the warring nations.

When the year's battles had ended, the gains and losses were small while the casualties had mounted into the hundreds of thousands. In the Somme fighting alone the British suffered as many as 60,000 casualties in a single day.

With the continued deadlock on the Western Front the Allies turned to the Mediterranean area. In April 1915 the British had sent an expedition of Australians and New Zealanders ("Anzacs") to the Gallipoli peninsula in an effort to defeat Turkey by gaining control of the straits of the Dardanelles. Here again sheer valor was no match for defensive weapons, and the problem of supplying a force so far from its base in England proved impossible to solve. Although the Gallipoli campaign ended in failure in 1916, one of the officials in London who was its champion would return to fight another day in another war. This was Britain's First Lord of the Admiralty at the start of World War I, who was to become his country's legendary Prime Minister in World War II: Winston Spencer Churchill. After the Dardanelles disaster Churchill resigned his Navy post and went to France as a lieutenant colonel with the Army.

The most important naval battle of World War I was also fought in 1916. This was the Battle of Jutland which began on May 31 in the North Sea off the western coast of Denmark and ended on June 1.

Up to this point the British Navy had swept German merchant ships from the seas. It also had kept the German battle fleet blockaded at Kiel. Now Germany's Admiral Reinhard Scheer decided to come out and risk a fight. The British fleet under Admiral Sir John Jellicoe met the challenge but lost several more ships and suffered many more casualties than the Germans.

This sea battle was hailed as a great victory in Germany. When it was over, however, the German fleet fled back to its safe anchorage and never fought again. Later in the war when it was once more ordered to sea, the crews mutinied.

Although Germany's surface fleet was no major threat to the Allies, its submarines were. German U-boats (from the word *Unterseebooten*) almost succeeded in starving England into submission by cutting her vital lifeline of food and supplies. A warning from President Woodrow Wilson resulted in Germany's modifying its campaign of unrestricted submarine warfare. Then on May 7, 1915, a U-boat torpedoed a British passenger liner, the *Lusitania,* off the Irish coast. The pride of England's merchant fleet sank in half an hour and 1,198 persons were drowned, 124 of whom were Americans. This act brought the United States to the brink of war.

President Wilson was determined, however, that America should remain neutral. In 1916 he was elected to a second term as President on the campaign slogan, "He Kept Us Out of War." The President did not speak for all Americans, however. Ex-President Theodore Roosevelt spoke out loudly and clearly in favor of declaring war on Germany. Many people agreed with him, although they did not quite agree with Roosevelt when he accused Wilson of being a "pussyfooter."

From the start of the war most Americans had reacted against Germany for its violation of Belgian neutrality. There were also other incidents that added fuel to the fires of the war party in the United States. One was the attempt made by the German foreign secretary, Alfred Zimmermann, to form an alliance between his country and Mexico. As a part of this bargain Zimmermann promised that Germany would see to it that Mexico was given the states of New Mexico, Arizona, and Texas. When this proposal became known to the public—the message was intercepted by the British and given to the United States —many Americans were more than ready for war.

Then in January 1917 Germany announced it was resuming unrestricted submarine warfare. The United States promptly delivered an ultimatum. Germany's one concession was the right for one United States ship a week to travel through the war zone if this ship was painted with zebra stripes of red and white. Most Americans regarded this as an insult.

On February 3, 1917, Wilson severed diplomatic relations with Germany. On March 27 it was announced that four American ships had been sunk by U-boats. Wilson then called for a special session of Congress to ask for a declaration of war. War was declared against Germany on April 6, 1917.

Three

Introducing
Billy Mitchell
and
Eddie Rickenbacker

A few days after General Pershing had established his headquarters in Paris an aide entered his office one morning to tell him he had a visitor.

"Who is it?" Pershing asked.

But the visitor did not have to be announced. He was already in the office. He saluted smartly and introduced himself.

General Pershing rose to return the salute.

"Sir," the major said before Pershing was all the way out of his chair, "I'd like to give you my ideas about how the A.E.F. Air Service should be set up."

Pershing hid a smile at the major's boyish enthusiasm. "Fine," he said. "But don't you think we should sit down first?"

"Yes, sir. Excuse me, sir." But without waiting to sit down the major launched right into all of his plans. He talked and acted as if he expected General Pershing to understand and approve everything he was proposing right then and there.

This dashing young major was William "Billy" Mitchell, who would one day become one of the most famous men in military aviation history.

Billy Mitchell had fought as a private in the Spanish-American war. After that war he had remained in the Army Signal Corps and rose rapidly through the ranks. In the early 1900's the Army bought its first airplanes for use by the Signal Corps. Most Army officers in those early days thought that airplanes might be used for observation work over enemy lines. Aside from that they couldn't see the airplane's military value. Billy Mitchell, however, had other ideas.

Mitchell had not learned to fly until 1916. As soon as he became a pilot, however, he began urging the Army to devote every effort toward developing the airplane as a weapon of war. Several months before America entered World War I Mitchell had come to Europe to see how France and Great Britain were using their airplanes on the Western Front. What he saw convinced him more than ever that the airplane was the war weapon of the future. It might even turn the tide in this war.

"Let me see if I understand you correctly," General Pershing said now. "What you want us to do is set up *both* a pursuit command and a bombardment command?"

"Yes, sir," Billy Mitchell said.

Pershing slowly shook his head. He was impressed with the dashing Billy Mitchell's enthusiasm. And he could see how fighter planes and observation planes might be of

Brigadier General William "Billy" Mitchell, Chief of the Air Service, A.E.F. (U.S. Army photograph).

some value. But planes for bombardment? It didn't make much sense. What was wrong with artillery, particularly the rapid-fire artillery that was now available?

Pershing recalled only too clearly that, when he had been sent into Mexico after Pancho Villa in 1916, an attempt to use airplanes had ended in complete disaster. There the 1st Aero Squadron's planes were blown about by high winds, could not fly over the mountains, and had to make forced landings far from their home base at Columbus, New Mexico. Not a single one of them had proved of any value against Villa. What good could they do here on the Western Front? He said as much now to Major Mitchell.

"But aircraft have been improved a great deal since then, sir," Mitchell said. Then he began to name some of the flyers who had already become famous in this war— men like Britain's Edward Mannock and Canada's Billy Bishop, Germany's Baron Manfred von Richthofen and France's René Fonck and Georges Guynemer.

Mannock was of the stuff from which legends are made. The son of a British regular army corporal, young Mannock had managed to become a pilot even though he had sight in but one eye. By the end of this year he would have shot down more than 50 German planes. He would not live, however, to receive the Victoria Cross he was awarded for the 73 victories he eventually tallied. Death lay ahead for Edward "Mickey" Mannock in the summer of 1918, and the King would present the Victoria Cross to the air hero's corporal father.

Billy Bishop was also well along toward tallying his record of 72 victories. Bishop's fabulous feats included 25 planes downed in 12 days. On his final day in the air in 1918 he would score five victories. He would live to receive the Victoria Cross and return to Canada and again serve his nation in World War II.

Baron von Richthofen, Germany's legendary Ace, was called "The Red Devil" by the Allied flyers who fought against him. He was the feared and respected leader of Richthofen's Flying Circus. The Richthofen Circus flew red-nosed Fokkers, while their leader flew a red Fokker triplane. Eventually Richthofen would shoot down 80 planes before he himself met his death in the air in April 1918.

France's René Fonck had led a charmed life so far in the war, and he was to continue to be one of the lucky ones. His final victory tally was to reach 73, but never during his two years of combat flying would he be even slightly wounded and few bullets would ever hit his plane. Fonck's comrade in aerial arms, Georges Guynemer, however, was to meet a far different fate.

Guynemer was idolized by the French people. He was a strange and lonely man suffering from severe lung trouble, and he seemed to know he was flying on borrowed time. His piercing black eyes seemed to look toward nothing but the sky and daily aerial combat. His record of victories had been growing steadily and would reach a final total of 53. Then, on September 11, 1917, the strange end would come: Guynemer would fly into combat never to return. Neither his plane nor his body would ever be found. The only ones who would seem to know what really happened to the beloved Georges Guynemer would be the French school children. They would say that he had simply flown so high in the sky that he was unable to return to earth. And so the story of Guynemer's last flight would grow until it became almost a myth that is still told in France today.

The names of these flyers and their combat records at this stage of the war were, of course, as familiar to Pershing as they were to Billy Mitchell. Combat pilots were a breed of men new to war, and everyone had become fascinated by the deeds of these warriors of the skies. In fact, the names of many flyers had become much better known than most of the army generals. Nevertheless Major Mitchell told about them in detail now to try and win his argument with General Pershing.

"These men and a dozen others have *proved* the airplane's a valuable war weapon, sir," Mitchell said. "The first new one besides the tank that has come out of this war."

"The men you've mentioned are all pursuit pilots," Pershing said. "I agree we should have pursuit ships."

Then Mitchell told Pershing about the success Britain's General Hugh "Boom" Trenchard had been having with bombardment by airplane far behind the enemy's front lines.

General Pershing waved his hand impatiently. "I'll recommend the pursuit and observation squadrons for the air service, but not the bombers. Not just yet, anyway." This was one of the few times in his army career that General Pershing was to be shortsighted. Later in the war he would approve both bomber and fighter planes, but never would he agree to set up a separate American strategic bomber command.

Major Mitchell had been a soldier long enough to recognize a firm no when he heard one. He rose now, saluted smartly, and said, "Thank you, sir." There was no note of discouragement in his voice. He was as much a born fighter as was Pershing, and he had just begun to fight.

As Billy Mitchell strode from the office, Pershing made a mental note to have him promoted to lieutenant colonel and appointed aviation officer of the A.E.F. Someone else, however, would have to be made commander of the American air service—someone who has a little more mature, a little less headstrong, and someone with a little more experience and rank. But was there anyone who could keep bouncing Billy Mitchell under control?

What was there about airplanes, Pershing wondered, that caused the men who flew them to become so dedicated to them? They seemed to love their planes the way cavalrymen loved their horses. Billy Mitchell wasn't the first person he had met who talked about flying as if it were a crusade. Young Eddie Rickenbacker, Pershing's staff car driver, was exactly the same way.

Just before Pershing had left the United States for France, Rickenbacker had tried to get officials in Washington interested in a pet aviation plan of his. Although still in his twenties, Rickenbacker was already famous as a racing car driver. He had won a number of races on dirt tracks all over the country and had driven in the big race at Indianapolis. Rickenbacker was sure he could get a number of his fellow racing drivers to join with him in forming a special squadron of combat flyers. No one in Washington seemed interested, however, and the young man was keenly disappointed.

In New York Pershing had suggested to Rickenbacker that he join the Army and come with him to France. He had leaped at the chance, but now that they were in France Pershing suspected it wouldn't be long before Rickenbacker would become a combat pilot. Pershing would hate to lose him because he knew more about motors than any half-dozen expert mechanics. But when a man was once bitten by the flying bug there seemed little else to do but let him fly.

With an effort Pershing forced any further thoughts about Billy Mitchell and Eddie Rickenbacker from his mind. He had other vital problems to solve. The air service was only one of a thousand matters that demanded his attention during these first trying weeks in France.

American manpower was his most urgent problem. If the United States delayed too long in raising a huge army, the Allies might lose the war before America could bring its weight to bear. Even a delay of a few weeks might be too long.

Now he asked his aide to come in.

"I want to send a cable to Newton Baker," Pershing said.

"Yes, sir."

The cable Pershing dictated read:

Plans should be made to send over at least 1,000,000 men by next May.

A few weeks later Pershing was to tell Newton Baker that in time the A.E.F. should total 3,000,000 men.

*   *   *

The United States Regular Army numbered just 135,000 men in the spring of 1917. As soon as war was declared many patriotic young Americans volunteered. In California on April 9 a 16-year-old lad by the name of Francis Scott Key Deuber joined the marines. Deuber was the great-great-grandson of the author of *The Star-Spangled Banner*. At Ann Arbor, Michigan, the University of Michigan football coach, Fielding H. "Hurry Up" Yost, cancelled spring practice and urged his players to "do a man's part in the defense of your country."

Newspapers featured such stories to help increase voluntary enlistments, and patriotism ran high. Many owners of German police dogs were reported as having changed their dogs' names from "Kaiser" to "Yank." The German Kaiser in fact became as much of a hated symbol as Hitler was to become in World War II. Many volunteers reported they were joining the Army "to get the Kaiser." Nevertheless it was soon clear that it would be necessary to draft men for duty in order to provide the millions of men General Pershing was asking for to win the war.

A Selective Service Act was passed on May 18, 1917. This Act authorized the President to increase the size of the Regular Army, to take the National Guard and National Guard Reserve into Federal service, and, most important of all: the President could raise an additional military force by selective draft. The draft came as a blow to Germany, who thought that the United States would depend upon volunteers for its army.

The United States had also used the draft during the Civil War. Then, however, it was a failure because a man who was drafted could send a substitute or buy his own exemption. In World War I Newton Baker decided to let local boards register men for the draft. They classified each man and decided whether or not he could be exempted. This made each man the direct responsibility of his own neighbors. The method worked so perfectly that it was again put into use at the start of World War II. More than 60 per cent of the A.E.F. were draftees as compared with about 2 per cent during the Civil War.

On June 5 some 9½ million men between the ages of 21 and 31 registered. On July 20 in Washington Secretary of War Newton Baker, wearing a blindfold, drew the first draft number from a large bowl. The number was 258. It was sent by telegraph to cities and towns all across the nation. Since there were 4,557 registration districts, with one man in each district being registered under the number 258, this meant 4,557 men were drafted on the first lottery drawing. The drawing then continued for 16½ hours, during which time 1,374,000 men were called to the colors to serve in the National Army. Some months later additional men between 18 and 45 were called up.

The methods to be used in training these hundreds of thousands of rookies presented General Pershing with one of his most serious problems.

Even before coming to France, General Pershing was firmly convinced that American infantry troops should be trained for fighting in an open style of warfare. The deadly stalemate on the Western Front had continued right up to 1917. Neither side had gained more than a dozen miles in all these months and years of futile fighting. Pershing knew that the siege of trench warfare must be broken, and the only way this could be done was to drive the enemy out of the trenches and into the open. This, he believed, American soldiers must be trained to do.

Pershing found, however, that the French and British disagreed with him.

But after an early tour of the front lines the Commander of the A.E.F. was more than ever convinced that his ideas were right. Here he saw with his own eyes how the men of both sides had been driven underground like animals by the machine gun and artillery. He saw how the fortresses that were the trenches on both sides faced each other for mile on endless mile. In some places these trenches were only yards apart. He saw the endless forest of barbed wire where attackers were trapped after they went "over the top," and made valiant yet futile efforts to cross the "No

Man's Land," that separated the friendly lines from the enemy lines. He knew only too well the terrible number of casualties that resulted from this kind of warfare. And it wasn't only when there were attacks that these losses took place. Day in and day out on the Western Front, the losses went on at a fearful rate of some 7,000 men a day. When actual battles occurred the casualties were much, much greater.

A typical example of the terrible Allied casualty rate was shown by the experience of a young British officer in the Grenadier Guards who fought in three major battles at the start of the war. His regiment went into the battle of Loos with some 30 or 40 officers and 600 to 800 men. They came out of that battle with about 100 men and three officers, of which the young Guardsman was one. They went into the next battle with about 600 men and 30 officers. They came out of it with one officer—the young Grenadier—and fewer than 100 men. In the third battle they again went in at full strength and came out with two officers and fewer than 100 men. This time, however, the young officer was severely wounded in the hip. This young Grenadier Guardsman was Harold Macmillan, who was to become Great Britain's Prime Minister in 1957.

A change in the style of fighting that resulted in such casualties simply had to be brought about. Pershing believed that American troops could make this change. Despite their great losses, however, the British and French refused to believe him. Nevertheless Pershing directed that American soldiers should be trained in open offensive warfare with the main emphasis placed on the use of the rifle and the bayonet.

On the average, draftees had six months of basic military training in the United States. When possible, their instructors included French and British veterans of the fighting on the Western Front. Pershing issued specific orders, however, that this instruction was to emphasize offensive, *not* defensive, methods of fighting. The men were also drilled in the fundamentals of army life—"the School of the Soldier," as it was called—and given as much physical training as possible to ready them for combat. Then they were shipped overseas.

One of Pershing's most important problems—that of actually transporting the A.E.F. safely to France—was one that he personally could not do too much about solving. This was a task for the United States Navy. It was a task that was placed in the good strong hands of as salty and capable a seaman as Pershing was a hard-grained and capable soldier. This man was Admiral William S. Sims.

Four

Introducing
William Sims

Just two years older than Pershing, Admiral Sims was every inch the man of action. His short gray beard gave him a dignified appearance, but he never let dignity stand in the way of what he regarded as his duty. He was gruff-voiced, and fearlessly outspoken. He had a temper that sometimes caused his face to grow quite red, but he also had a rare sense of humor. His dark, flashing eyes had made more than one junior officer tremble in his presence. Admiral Sims had made countless friends during his long years at sea—and not a few enemies.

Shortly after America went to war, Admiral Sims arrived in England. He immediately met with Britain's First Sea Lord, Admiral Jellicoe, veteran of the Battle of Jutland. The news Jellicoe had to report was not good. German submarines had sunk more than half a million tons of merchant shipping in February, more than that in March, and it looked like a million tons of shipping would be sunk in April.

"These figures are worse than those you've been giving the public," Sims said.

"Far worse," Jellicoe agreed. "Right now there is only a three-week supply of grain in the whole of England."

"What you're saying is that if we don't lick the submarine the submarine will lick us."

Jellicoe nodded. "Unless the submarine can be conquered," he said grimly, "the Royal Navy predicts defeat by late autumn."

Sims accepted the words at their face value. He knew the British were not given to exaggeration. Nor were they apt to panic, no matter how great the odds. Sims himself had been born in Canada, and he had always greatly admired the British. In fact back in 1910 he had got into a great deal of hot water by making a speech in which he said that if the British Empire were ever threatened by an enemy, they could "count on the assistance of every man, every ship, every dollar from the United States." German statesmen had kicked up a row about that speech, and President William Howard Taft had told him not to make such public statements again. The British, of course, had loved every word of it. Maybe he could now count on some of that good will he had built up with them. After all the submarine had to be licked, not just to make the seas safe for merchant ships but for troopships that would be carrying the A.E.F. to France. And he thought he knew the way to do the job.

"I think the submarine can be licked," Sims said now.

Jellicoe looked interested. "And just how?"

"By using a convoy system."

As Sims had expected, Jellicoe disagreed. The British

Admiral William S. Sims, Commander, United States Naval Forces Operating in European Waters during World War I. (Navy Department photograph in the National Archives).

had never liked the idea of having groups of ships sail together in a convoy, because of the possibility of collisions. This possibility was increased at night when the ships had to sail without lights. In addition, a convoy of merchant ships or troopships had to be protected by cruisers and destroyers, and the Royal Navy did not feel it had any of these to spare.

"The United States can lend a considerable hand with destroyers and cruisers," Admiral Sims said.

Admiral Jellicoe said he still did not like the idea.

Sims' voice was firm, his voice hard. "I believe we're going to have to try it," he said.

Jellicoe's eyes grew frosty at the challenge in Sims' voice. The First Sea Lord was not used to having people disagree with him. But he knew Sims' ideas were not to be taken lightly. He had invented a system for firing ships' guns that had been adopted by all the navies of the world, including the Royal Navy. It was this system that had made it possible for the United States Navy to establish truly remarkable records in shooting at targets. Sims was also recognized throughout the world as an expert in many other kinds of naval warfare.

Suddenly Jellicoe smiled. "Perhaps we should give it a try," he said.

The two men rose and shook hands.

Less than a month later the first American destroyers that Admiral Sims had promised arrived in England. British Admiral Sir Lewis Bayly asked Commander Taussig of the American command how soon his destroyers would be ready to return to sea. Bayly expected that Taussig would want his men to have several days' rest after their rough Atlantic crossing.

"We'll be ready for escort duty just as soon as our ships

can be refueled," Taussig said. This took only a few hours.

The first trial convoy of merchant ships sailed from Gibraltar in May 1917. Escorted by destroyers and submarine chasers, the convoy arrived safely in London on May 20. Soon afterward the system was used for all ships crossing the Atlantic. The first convoys were made up of from six to eight ships with their escorts. In time there were as many as 40 or 50 ships in a convoy.

The 1st Division of the A.E.F. sailed from New York in mid-June. It was escorted by American warships to within about 100 miles of the French coast. There additional British destroyers escorted the convoy into port at St. Nazaire. Several submarine attacks were made on the ships, but there were no casualties. The success of this voyage proved that the entire A.E.F. could be safely transported to Europe from the United States.

One of the reasons the United States Navy could move so swiftly into action was that its staff officers and other naval officials in Washington had been preparing for war long before America's entry into the conflict. One of these officials was the assistant to Josephus Daniels, Secretary of the Navy. This able young man would one day become the nation's President and Commander-in-Chief of all its armed forces during World War II. He was Franklin D. Roosevelt.

Young Roosevelt had been assistant Secretary of the Navy since 1913. Before the war he had worked hard and long to enlarge the Navy shipyards and make them more efficient. When the United States entered the war there were about 75,000 men in its naval forces. Roosevelt helped recruit men to increase this number to more than 500,000. He also helped Admiral Sims defeat the German U-boats by suggesting that special types of mines be laid in a belt between Norway and the Orkney Islands. This closed the English Channel and North Sea to marauding submarines.

By the end of 1917 the "bridge of ships" built across the Atlantic by the United States and Great Britain was landing some 50,000 men a month in Europe. By the spring of 1918 this figure rose to about 100,000 men a month, and in July of that year a record 300,000 men were landed. The United States used not only its own ships for troop transports but also German passenger liners that had been interned in American ports at the start of the war. The British provided all of the liners they could spare to carry American troops. By the end of the war they had actually carried more American soldiers than had the United States. The United States, however, provided almost all of the naval escorts for the transports. So successful was the work of the American Cruiser and Transport Force that of the more than 2,000,000 men carried to France only 100 were lost when the transport *Ticonderoga* was sunk by a German U-boat.

The greatest troop carrier was the *Leviathan*. This was the former German ship *Vaterland*. Seized by America in 1917 and re-equipped as a transport, it landed 12,000 men of the A.E.F. in France every month. The *Great Northern* and the *Northern Pacific* were the fastest transports, making round trips in an average of 19 days.

None of the men of the A.E.F. who sailed to Europe aboard a troop transport ever forgot the experience. Most of them had never been on a ship before, and many of them had never even been away from home. Now, suddenly, they found themselves jammed together by the hundreds in airless compartments several decks below the ship's waterline. Occasionally they would be brought up on deck for a quick breath of fresh air. These brief moments on deck were like reprieves. The men then had a chance to see the rest of the convoy—the other transports sailing majestically nearby, their flanks protected by the terrier-like destroyers with their death-dealing depth charges ready to be dropped at the first warning of the sighting of a submarine. All too soon, however, the men would be herded back below decks where each soldier had to fight his own personal battle against homesickness, seasickness, and the fear of a sudden blow from an enemy torpedo.

American soldiers hated the German U-boats because there seemed no way to fight back against their sudden, silent onslaught. Thus the news that one of the underwater killers had been destroyed was always greeted with great enthusiasm.

On November 17, 1917, the United States Navy struck one such blow that spread joy among all the men of the A.E.F. On that day eight American destroyers were leading a convoy through submarine-infested waters just off the Irish coast. Suddenly the men aboard the destroyer *Fanning* spotted a U-boat periscope. They knew that an attack was about to be launched against one of the ships in the convoy they were escorting.

Lieutenant Walter Henry, deck officer of the *Fanning,* immediately depth-charged the U-boat. Commander Frank Berrien of the destroyer *Nicholson* also joined his ship in the depth-charging attack. The other destroyers gave support by shelling the area where the periscope had been sighted.

After this swift defensive flurry silence fell across the sea while the Americans watched and waited. The destroyers' crews were certain they had driven off the U-boat, but they had hoped they might even have accomplished more than that. As the silence continued the men's disappointment grew. They decided the U-boat had escaped.

Then, right before their startled eyes, the German *U-58* boiled up out of the ocean depths. When it had completely surfaced, its conning tower opened and its crew came tumbling out offering to surrender. They were allowed to swim to the *Fanning*, where they were taken on board. There they explained that the hull of their submarine had not been damaged but the depth charges had wrecked the navigation gear. Kapitän Amberger, commander of the *U-58*, had decided to surface and surrender his submarine rather than risk suffocation for himself and his crew.

The *U-58* was the first enemy submarine captured by the United States Navy.

Getting the men to France was, of course, only a part of the Navy's tremendous job. Supplies and equipment in unbelievable quantities also had to be carried across the Atlantic. Between 50 and 60 pounds of supplies and equipment per man had to be landed on every day that a member of the A.E.F. landed in France. This amounted to some 25 to 30 carloads of supplies daily for each combat division. Late in the war about nine million pounds of food daily were being brought ashore in France. In order to carry this food across France once it was landed, many thousands of freight cars and steam locomotives were also transported from the United States.

The organization in charge of providing food and equipment for the A.E.F. was called the Services of Supply (S.O.S.). Commander of the S.O.S. was General James G. Harbord. Its purchasing agent in the United States was

Charles G. Dawes, who later became Vice President of the United States under President Calvin Coolidge.

On the home front most civilians were more than willing to deny themselves the kinds and quantities of food they had been used to eating if their sacrifice meant that the boys "Over There" would get more and better food as a result. Herbert Hoover, future United States President, was named Food Administrator. Special wheatless and meatless days were observed. Bakers tried making bread from alfalfa flour, and loyal citizens tried to eat it and like it despite its greenish color. As another patriotic gesture sauerkraut was renamed "Liberty Cabbage."

Harry A. Garfield, son of ex-President James Garfield, was named Fuel Administrator, and took charge of the national production and consumption of coal. To save fuel and electricity and to provide more daylight hours in the evening, the government decided to try having everyone move their clocks forward one hour. The plan was called "Daylight Saving," and had first been suggested as far back as the 18th century by Benjamin Franklin. The British had found the plan successful early in World War I, but American farmers did not like it. They said Daylight Saving Time upset the routine of farm work.

"Cows can't read clocks," they pointed out, meaning that cows had to be milked at their regular milking time no matter what time the clock said it was.

The farmers, of course, did not need any special encouragement to do their jobs. "Food Will Win the War" was their slogan, and they were willing to be in the fields from sun-up until after dark working to provide the bumper crops to prove it. Sometimes farmers were assisted by volunteer women and children from nearby towns. Also to provide more food the nation's Boy Scouts made a special project of planting and tending and harvesting their own vegetable gardens. These patriotic young men, many of whom had fathers and brothers and uncles serving with the A.E.F., adopted a special slogan for their national project:

EVERY SCOUT TO FEED A SOLDIER!

Five

*"You
May Insist
All You
Please . . . !"*

General Pershing moved his headquarters from Paris to Chaumont on September 1, 1917. From here he and his staff directed the final pre-combat training of American troops who were now arriving in France daily. It was at this point that the commander of the A.E.F. had his second sharp disagreement with the French and British.

The French and British were in desperate need of manpower. They assumed that American troops would be used as piecemeal replacements to fill out losses in existing French and British divisions. While he was deeply sympathetic with the Allies and the losses they had suffered, Pershing felt this method of using American soldiers would be turning them into cannon fodder. He believed that American troops must be commanded only by Americans.

He also felt that they should go into battle as separate and distinct American units, not merely used here and there as scattered replacements.

In both decisions Pershing was opposed strongly by England's Prime Minister, David Lloyd George, France's Premier, Georges Clemenceau, as well as by Britain's Sir Douglas Haig and France's Ferdinand Foch. Nevertheless Pershing held his ground, and he was backed up by President Wilson and War Secretary Newton Baker. They had picked a man in whom they had every confidence to command the A.E.F. and they saw no reason to change their minds now. Pershing's War Department directive on this subject read:

"In military operations against the Imperial German Government you are directed to cooperate with the forces of the other countries employed against the enemy; but in so doing the underlying idea must be kept in view that the forces of the United States are a separate and distinct component of the combined forces, the identity of which must be preserved. . . . The decision as to when your command or any of its parts is ready for action is confided to you, and you will exercise full discretion in determining the manner of cooperation."

Pershing held to this directive as well as to his own convictions in spite of any and all opposition: Americans would fight as American units, commanded by Americans. Pershing was a person rarely given to anger, but on at least one occasion he declared himself on this point in no uncertain terms to Marshal Foch. This incident took place at an Allied conference when Foch told Pershing to yield his command by placing American troops under French leaders.

Pershing objected.

"I must insist upon this arrangement," Foch said.

Pershing's fist crashed down on the conference table. "Marshal Foch," he said, "you may insist all you please, but I decline absolutely to agree to your plan!"

Pershing knew, of course, that no time could be wasted in getting the A.E.F. into action. The year that America entered the war was a year of near disaster for the Allies, making it imperative that United States troops be readied for combat just as soon as possible.

In the early spring of 1917 revolution had broken out in Russia. In November the new Bolshevik government asked the Central Powers for an armistice. Russia and Germany signed a peace treaty in March 1918. Some 4,000 men of the American 85th Division were sent to Murmansk to prevent the Bolsheviks from taking over Allied military supplies stored there. Later an additional 10,000 men from the United States 27th and 31st Infantry Regiments were sent to Vladivostok to protect the trans-Siberian railroad.

In October 1917 the Italians suffered a major defeat at Caporetto with losses of several hundred thousand men. Later the United States 332nd Infantry regiment was sent to Italy to bolster morale. Italy remained in the war but never recovered from the Caporetto disaster. Thus the Germans were able to transfer many divisions from both the Eastern and Italian Fronts to fight on the Western Front.

Meanwhile there was a series of mutinies by war-weary French troops. This put the main combat effort squarely up to the British, who responded magnificently as they had throughout the war. The results, however, were tragic. British casualties during the long, savage battle for Passchendaele Ridge in Belgium amounted to a quarter of a million men. At Cambrai the British scored a limited but important success with an attack that was spearheaded by about 400 tanks.

Early in 1917 the Germans withdrew to the Hindenburg Line. This line of defenses was so strong that some Allied leaders thought it would be impossible to break through it. Pershing, however, continued to have the A.E.F. trained for the open attack with rifle and bayonet, no matter how strong the defenses appeared to be.

By the end of the year there were five American divisions in France. These included the 1st Division, made up of United States Army regulars who had been the first to arrive at St. Nazaire; the 26th Division, whose members were New England National Guardsmen; the 2nd Division, which was a combination of Army men and Marines; the 42nd Division, which was called the Rainbow Division because it was made up of National Guard units from almost all of the states of the Union; and the 41st Division, made up of National Guard units from the Northwestern part of the United States. Early in 1918 the arrival of the 32nd Division brought the total number of American divisions in France to six. During the course of the war some 93 combat divisions were organized. Forty-two of these reached France, and 30 saw active combat. An A.E.F. division had 979 officers and 27,082 men. This was more than twice the size of the British and French divisions, which numbered about 12,000 and 11,000 men respectively. German combat divisions numbered slightly more than 12,000 men.

The first American casualties in France were not killed in combat but at a hospital at Dannes-Camiers on September 4, 1917, when the hospital was hit by German bombs. These men were Lieutenant William Fitzsimmons,

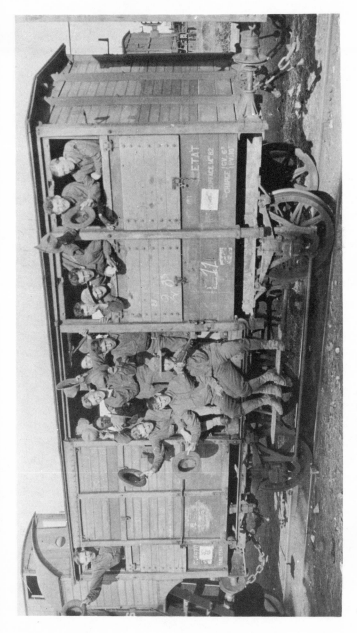

U.S. doughboys are shown leaving St. Nazaire, France, for a training camp. These box cars could carry either 40 men or 8 horses (HOMMES 40, CHEVAUX 8) and were often called "Side-door Pullmans" by the men of the A.E.F. (U.S. Signal Corps photograph in the National Archives).

Kansas City, Mo., Private Oscar C. Tugo, Boston, Mass.; Private Leslie D. Woods, Streator, Ill.; and Private Rudolph Rubino, New York City.

The first battle casualties of an American unit while serving at the front were Sergeant Matthew Calderwood and Private William Branigan of the 11th Engineers. They were wounded by shellfire while working on a railway near Gouzeaucourt on September 5, 1917.

On October 20 the 1st Division entered the front lines near Lunéville, a town that the hard-bitten Army regulars promptly nicknamed, "Looneyville." The Americans, however, were not the only ones to use nicknames. For a time the British Tommies called their American brothers-in-arms "Sammies," but this was a nickname that never quite caught on. American soldiers were generally called "Yanks," a term that many of them did not like. They were also called "doughboys." The exact origin of this term is unknown, although it probably came from the fact that Federal troops in the American Civil War had big round brass buttons on their uniforms. These buttons resembled "Doughboys," which are dumplings or pieces of fried dough.

The first American artillery shot of World War I was fired on October 23 by Battery C of the 1st Division's 6th Field Artillery. Sergeant Alexander Arch was in charge of the squad firing the gun. After the war this historic field piece was returned to the United States to be kept as a trophy at West Point.

To the 1st Division also went a more tragic "first." On November 2 some 250 German storm troops conducted a trench raid on a single 1st Division platoon near Bathelemont, killing three men. These were the first Americans killed in the trenches. The men were Corporal James B. Gresham, Evansville, Ind.; Private Thomas F. Enright, Pittsburgh, Pa.; and Private Merle D. Hay, Ellston, Iowa.

The first major offensive in which American troops took part was the Cambrai campaign between November 20 and December 4, 1917. The 11th, 12th, and 14th Engineer Regiments were serving behind the British lines when this campaign began, and were soon caught up in the combat action.

As the other American infantry divisions completed their advanced training they too were sent into the trenches. Although every effort was made to send these green troops into quiet sectors, these divisions also began to suffer their first casualties, and the grim toll of war began to be felt not only at the front but in lonely homes all across the face of America.

Many doughboys felt, however, that actual combat above ground was not nearly so grim as day-to-day life below ground in the trenches. Most trenches and dugouts were wet and cold even in good weather. When it rained, which it seemed to do most of the time at the front, the walls and floors would be awash with water. The only light was provided by feeble candle flames, and these often went out in the foul air. The men also lived in constant fear of the sounding of the klaxon announcing a gas attack.

"We're living in the dark underground with the snails," was the way one Yank described it in a letter home. "A few days of this and you begin to wish for 'Zero Hour' and an attack against the Hun. Actually the Hun seems to be the least of our problems. In addition to the snails coming out of the dugout walls when it rains we have trench rats visiting us nightly. They can shred leather shoes like lettuce. And then we have another interesting little critter: the 'Cootie.' Cooties [body lice] are always with us. We've even made up a song about them. It goes:

> *You're in the army now,*
> *You're not behind the plow,*
> *You'll never get rich,*
> *You've got the itch,*
> *You're in the army now."*

In the spring of 1918 the Germans launched an all-out drive to win the war, and every available American fighting man in France was soon called upon to help stem this fierce attack.

The German spring offensive was started on March 21 and was aimed at Amiens. It soon became clear that the purpose of the drive was to destroy the British Army by separating the British-held Somme front from the French front further south. Within a few days a wedge or *salient* (the part of a battle line that extends sharply to the front of the general line) was driven between the two armies. The Germans also drove to a point near Amiens.

Early in April the Germans launched a second mass attack against the British in Flanders. The Allies were now faced with their greatest crisis since the German drive in the opening weeks of the war. For more than two years since then the opposing armies had been measuring successful attacks in yards. Suddenly, however, the Germans had now advanced some 40 miles.

Two all-important events took place at this time. The Allies made General Ferdinand Foch Commander-in-Chief of the Allied Armies, and General Pershing proved he was a man who was big enough and unselfish enough

Many Yanks were rushed into battle by motor transport to stem the German drive in the spring and summer of 1918. (U.S. Army photograph).

to be able to change his mind when it was important to others that he do so. Pershing still believed that American units should keep their identities as American units and that they should be sent into battle only under American leaders. But he also realized that this was a turning point in the war. If he continued to insist on having his own way during this major crisis, he might very well win his argument while the Allies lost the war. Pershing went to Foch and said:

"I come to say to you that the American people would hold it a great honor for our troops were they engaged in the present battle. I ask it of you in my name and in that of the American people. There is at this moment no other question than that of fighting. Infantry, artillery, aviation —all that we have are yours to dispose of as you will. Others are coming which are as numerous as will be necessary. I have come to say to you that the American people would be proud to be engaged in the greatest battle in history."

Pershing's words were widely reported in newspapers throughout the world, and they sent a thrill through the weary Allies at home and at the front.

It was mainly the British, however, who bore the brunt of these first two German drives of 1918. On April 12 Sir Douglas Haig issued a special order to all ranks of the British army demanding that "every position must be held to the last man. There must be no retirement. . . . Each one of us must fight to the end." And once more the heroic Tommies died where they stood to stop the German advance.

During this German offensive troops of the 26th Division were the first Americans to take part in a combat action that reached true battle proportions. This was at

U.S. infantrymen proved to be expert sharpshooters with either the British Enfield rifle or the American Springfield. Many men were also equipped with the less accurate French CHAUCHAT auto-rifles, which the Yanks called "Show-Shows." (U.S. Signal Corps photograph in the National Archives).

Seicheprey on April 20 when the 26th suffered more than 600 casualties in a dawn attack by several thousand Germans.

When the drives on the Somme front and in Flanders failed to reach their final objectives, the Germans launched a third attack along the Aisne River between Soissons and Reims. This area was known as the Chemin des Dames. By May 31 this surprise attack was so successful that the Germans had reached Château-Thierry on the Marne River just 40 miles from Paris. Once more, as it had in 1914, the French capital seemed about to fall. Many citizens fled the city and the government made plans to move.

The state of near panic was heightened by the fact that Paris was being mysteriously bombarded by artillery shells fired from a gun of fantastically long range. Paris had not been shelled since the Franco-Prussian War. During that dreadful siege over a million cannon balls had been fired into the capital, and now the French were fearful of an even worse rain of destruction.

The mysterious long-range gun, which the Yanks and Tommies nicknamed "Big Bertha," had begun its bombardment of Paris back in March. The fact that its shells began to fall on the city at the same time as the first German attacks had begun in the spring offensive seemed a dark omen to the French. The bombardment had continued off and on during the first successful German attacks but had ended in May. There had been no further shelling for almost a month, but now, with the German armies on the Marne and threatening the capital, Big Bertha had once again begun its deadly bombardment. Paris was a frightened city.

Six

Introducing
Big
Bertha

Saturday morning, March 23, 1918, dawned bright and clear in Paris. People rose early and immediately went marketing. Later in the day the shops would be out of food. As they stood in the long food queues, the people talked about the German offensive that had begun two days earlier against the British armies of Generals Gough and Byng in the north. The first reports of German successes sounded ominous to the war-tried people of Paris.

Now even more disturbing rumors began to be heard in the streets. Paris was being bombarded! *C'est impossible!* Bombardment was impossible. The German armies were 75 miles from Paris. True, the city *might* be shelled by artillery, but not until the Germans got within 25 or 30 miles.

An air raid then? There had been no enemy planes in the sky.

During the day some 25 shells fell on Paris. They fell at regular intervals, further ruling out the possibility of aerial bombardment. Sixteen persons were killed and 29 wounded. The actual damage, however, was not in physical casualties. The mystery gun was a major threat to civilian morale. And if the people behind the lines were thrown into a panic, what might not happen to the soldiers in the trenches? Already there had been trouble on that score with the mutinies and desertions of the previous year.

To prevent such panic, the French government announced through the Paris newspapers that the bombs on March 23 had been dropped by German aircraft.

The fear felt by the French people when the artillery shells began to fall was no mere accident. It had been planned this way by the German high command. It was part of a campaign of "frightfulness" (*schrechlichkeit*) to destroy civilian morale. The bombardment of Paris by long-range artillery had been scheduled to start at the same time as the attacks of the German armies in the spring offensive. The entire program was planned to win the war before American troops could go into combat and perhaps turn the tide of battle.

The second day of the bombardment fell on Palm Sunday. Many people were killed and wounded on their way to church.

Now there was no further attempt to pretend that the destruction was caused by aerial bombs. Impossible as it seemed, Paris was being shelled by a gun with a range of more than 75 miles. American newspapers such as the Chicago *Tribune* and the New York *Times* announced the news of Big Bertha's attacks to their startled readers. In London a famous astronomer, Charles Nordmann, was called upon to give his theories on how shells could be fired for such long distances and accurately hit a target, even as large a target as Paris. Nordmann and experts in other fields reviewed the whole history of the use of artillery, hoping to cast some light on this most recent development.

They recalled that the Turks had used a kind of cannon in attacking Constantinople as far back as the 15th century. These so-called "bombards" hurled huge stones that finally broke down the walls of the fortress. More recently the Germans had destroyed the fortresses at Liége and Namur with long-range guns called howitzers at the start of the war in 1914. And in 1915 Dunkirk had been bombarded by the Germans from a distance of about 25 miles.

Most German guns were manufactured at plants owned by the Krupp family. It was generally known among Allied soldiers and newspapermen that the head of this family was Frau Bertha von Bohlen. Thus the German long-range Paris gun got its nickname.

Big Bertha's most damaging blow fell on March 29, which was Good Friday. Late in the afternoon a shell struck the Church of St. Gervais, killing 80 and wounding 68 worshippers. Among the Belgian, French, British, and American casualties were civilian men, women, and children as well as a number of soldiers. Righteous wrath rose to a new high in the Allied world after this attack. Demands grew that the gun be found and destroyed.

This, of course, was exactly what the Allied high command was trying to do. A constant air search had been going on to find the site of Big Bertha ever since it had first started firing. It was believed that this site was in a forest near Laon. Air attacks in this area, however, had apparently been unsuccessful because the bombardment continued.

The long-range gun continued to fire its shells into the French capital throughout the month of April, the attacks taking place about every two or three days. Then, for no known reason, Big Bertha suddenly was silent for most of the month of May. The people of Paris had hoped and prayed that this meant the end of their ordeal.

Their prayers now seemed in vain, however, when in late May the German offensive on the Marne began and Big Bertha's attacks were resumed.

It was at this stage of the war that American fighting men first came into their own. On May 28 some 4,000 men of the 1st Division attacked the Germans at Cantigny. The veteran American regulars quickly drove the Germans from their strongly held positions. Then the Yanks dug in and held their ground in the face of seven vicious counterattacks during the next three days. News of this first success by the attack-minded Americans spread like wildfire and brought new hope to the hard-pressed Allies.

One of the heroes of the Cantigny attack was Major Theodore Roosevelt, Jr., oldest son of ex-President Theodore Roosevelt. At the start of the war ex-President Roosevelt had wanted to raise a volunteer division and lead it himself in France. This proposal had been turned down by War Secretary Baker, and the old "Rough Rider" never got to take part in the World War I combat. His four sons, however, more than lived up to the Roosevelt reputation as fighters.

Early in the war Kermit joined the British Army and was awarded the Military Cross for gallantry in action. He was later discharged from the British Army so that he could join the American Army, in which he became an artillery captain.

Archibald was an infantry captain and was seriously wounded by shrapnel in March 1918. Before he was rescued he lay in the muddy battlefield for 14 hours. He was finally invalided home with a paralyzed arm.

Theodore was decorated for his heroic actions at Cantigny. Before the war ended he became a lieutenant colonel, was gassed, severely wounded, and decorated more than two dozen times. In World War II he was to become a brigadier general and one of the great heroes of Omaha Beach during the Normandy invasion.

The fourth Roosevelt son to serve in World War I was Quentin, who was a lieutenant in the 95th Aero Pursuit Squadron. Quentin was extremely popular with his fellow flyers. Part of his popularity was due to his natural warmth and charm. Much of it, however, was due to the fact that he refused to accept any special treatment just because he was the son of an ex-President.

When Quentin reported for combat duty in France he was immediately made a flight commander. He refused the honor, saying it should go to one of the veteran flyers in the 95th. Later his superior officers ordered him to act as flight commander. Quentin then had no choice but to accept the role, but he quietly told the men with whom he was to fly that once they were in the air the one with the most experience was to assume command.

Quentin shot down his first German plane almost by accident. Returning from a patrol over the German lines, he joined up with what he thought was a formation of American planes. Suddenly the formation maneuvered and Quentin saw that the planes all had German Maltese crosses on their tails and wings. Instantly Quentin fired a burst from his machine guns into the German plane immediately ahead of him. It went down in flames and young Roosevelt sped for home. He regarded this incident as a great joke and seemed to enjoy telling the story about his almost-fatal blunder.

On July 14, 1918, Quentin and four other members of the 95th squadron, all of whom were flying Nieuports, attacked seven red-nosed Fokkers from Richthofen's Flying Circus. In the fierce dogfight that followed, Quentin was shot down in flames by Sergeant Karl Thom who had 24 previous victories to his credit. Quentin fell near Chamery, France, and the Germans buried him there, marking his grave with the wheels from his plane and a rude wooden cross inscribed:

ROOSEVELT, AMERICAN AVIATOR

When the news reached the United States, President Wilson sent a message of deep sympathy to ex-President Roosevelt. The blow was a particular bitter one to Quentin's father, because it was he who had first brought aviation to the attention of the United States Army in 1907. Although Orville and Wilbur Wright had flown their first airplane at Kitty Hawk, North Carolina, on December 17, 1903, it was not until 1907 that anyone in the United States seemed to think that there might be a possible military use for the airplane. And it was President Roosevelt who had then told his Secretary of War, William H. Taft, to look into the possibilities of having the Army buy a plane from the Wright brothers. It was out of this early negotiation that the World War I American Air

Service grew, the Air Service in which Quentin Roosevelt was to die.

*   *   *

Despite the American success at Cantigny, the Allied situation on the Marne at Château-Thierry remained critical. But here too, in a series of savage engagements, some 28,000 recklessly brave Americans played heroic roles.

The 3rd Division was in training near Chaumont when the German attack approached the Marne. It was ordered to Château-Thierry immediately. Machine-gun units were ordered forward by truck transport. These men drove for two days without sleep; and when they arrived at the Marne, they had to undergo two more days of artillery bombardment. Nevertheless they set up their machine guns and prevented the Germans from crossing the Marne bridges.

The 2nd Division was called upon by Marshal Foch to prevent the Germans from traveling down the Paris-Metz highway to the French capital. In order to reach their battle positions along the Paris road the Army and Marine units of the 2nd Division had to make their way forward through crowds of retreating French troops and civilian refugees who told the Americans the war was lost. The Yanks, however, moved forward—not merely to defend but to attack. And in the next two weeks the attack that the United States Marine Brigade of the 2nd Division made on Belleau Wood caused that grim battleground to become a legendary symbol of American wartime heroism.

Belleau Wood was not merely a well-defended German position. It was one solid wall of machine guns. The

Marines moved forward without even the benefit of an artillery barrage before the opening attack. As they advanced against this rain of death, the Marines bent forward like men leaning against a hurricane wind.

"Schrechlichkeit!" a veteran spat. "These Boche want frightfulness, we'll give it to them!"

And Sergeant Daniel Daly urged his men forward with the shout: "C'mon, you Leathernecks, you wanta live forever?"

For twenty-four hours a day during the next two weeks the Marines fought their way a savage yard at a time through this nightmare forest. Losses were enormous, yet no thought was given to retreat.

On June 26 the following famous message was received by General Pershing:

"Entire woods now occupied by United States Marines."

And a few days later the French published an official order stating that Belleau Wood was to be renamed the Wood of the Marines.

*   *   *

On July 15 Germany launched an attack on both sides of Reims that developed into the Second Battle of the Marne. This time the Germans were successful in crossing the Marne at Château-Thierry, but they were quickly hurled back. Some 85,000 Americans in the 3rd, 26th, 28th, and 42nd Divisions took part in this gallant Allied stand.

Once the initial German drive was stopped, the Allies went over to the offensive as they had been planning to do for some weeks. The main purpose of this Allied drive was to force the Germans from the Marne salient and thus end the threat to Paris.

Two American divisions, the 1st and 2nd, were given the honor of spearheading an attack on Soissons. In other areas of this offensive the following divisions also took part: 3rd, 4th, 26th, 28th, 32nd, 42nd, and 77th. In all there were several hundred thousand Americans engaged in the Second Battle of the Marne, which ended with complete success on August 6 when the Germans were forced to retreat beyond the Vesle River.

Seven

Death
Of
A Poet

But these American successes were not without cost. Some 50,000 young Americans died or were wounded in the Second Battle of the Marne. Among those who died was a young sergeant in the 42nd or Rainbow Division who was world-famous for a poem he had written shortly before the war. The young sergeant had also written several war poems—"Rouge Bouquet," "The White Ships and the Red," and others—that had been widely reprinted. But now he would write no more. He lay dead near the heights of the Ourcq River which the Rainbow Division had so valiantly stormed.

The idea for an American division made up of men from all over the United States had been War Secretary Newton Baker's. He had suggested it to General Pershing during their first meeting in Washington in 1917, and

Pershing had given it his stamp of approval. The Rainbow Division, as it was soon called, was made up of National Guard units from 26 states and the District of Columbia.

One of these National Guard units was New York's famous old "Fighting 69th." Shortly after the Fighting 69th had been called into Federal service, the young poet joined its ranks.

Most of the men of the Rainbow Division had never met a poet before, and they weren't at all sure they wanted to. But they soon learned to like this young man. For one thing he didn't *act* like a poet. A thoroughly charming person, he kept his comrades-in-arms entertained with tall stories of his work as a New York newspaperman. He also loved to talk about food. In fact to hear him tell it he seemed to enjoy eating more than writing poetry. One of his favorite meals during peacetime was steak for breakfast!

These tales about food were in even greater demand when the Rainbow Division got to France. There they were fed hardtack and French rations of canned meat-and-carrots which the Yanks called "monkey meat." They also were fed canned salmon, which they called "goldfish," and canned beef, which they called "corn willie." After such fare all of his friends wanted the young man to wax poetical about the meals he had loved to eat back in civilian life. He was only too happy to oblige.

But the young poet had his serious side too. The other men often heard him speak fondly of his wife and their three children, Deborah, Kenton, and Michael. There had also been another little daughter named Rose, who had died of polio, and the young poet grew sad when he spoke of her.

The Rainbow Division arrived at St. Nazaire on October 31, 1917. They went into the front lines in mid-February, 1918. On March 5 they suffered their first casualties, one officer and 18 men killed and 22 wounded when they were hit by a German trench raid.

A few days later the Rainbow men retaliated. They went over the top in the dead of night on a trench raid of their own. They captured several prisoners and suffered only slight losses. One of these prisoners was captured by a colonel wearing a private's uniform and carrying a .45 automatic. For this effort Colonel Douglas MacArthur, who one day would become one of the great heroes of World War II in the Pacific Theater of War, was awarded the French Croix de Guerre.

When the March 1918 German offensive began the Rainbow Division took over the Baccarat area. It was the first American unit to occupy a divisional sector. Soon they were a "blooded" division, veterans of combat upon whom Commander-in-Chief Foch could depend completely. They learned many lessons of war, and in turn they taught the Germans a few. For one thing they taught the Germans a lesson in accurate rifle fire. Captured German prisoners who had faced the Rainbow Division admitted they had never encountered such accurate shooting. A time or two when the Germans advanced against the Rainbow they were under the impression they were facing machine-gun fire when actually it was unbelievably rapid and accurate rifle fire.

One lesson the Rainbow men learned was one all of the other American divisions learned in time. This was not to advance in a body against machine-gun nests. The first time or two they tried this their casualties were

Sergeant Joyce Kilmer, the soldiers' poet. (U.S. Signal Corps photograph in the National Archives).

enormous. Then it occurred to these 20th-century soldiers to revert to fighting methods first taught their pioneer forefathers in America by the Indians. After that one man at a time would crawl forward on his stomach while his fellow soldiers "covered" him with rifle fire. When the first man had inched forward a few yards, then another man crawled forward, and another, and another until they were all within a few yards of the machine-gun nest. They would then capture the nest with a sudden last-minute rush.

They were wily old soldiers when they were called upon to take part in the Battle of the Ourcq, and among the wiliest of them all was the young poet. By now he was a sergeant and enormously proud of the fact. He would rather be a sergeant in the Rainbow Division, he was reported to have said, than a general in any other division.

The sergeant's battalion commander was Major William J. "Wild Bill" Donovan, who would become head of the famed Office of Strategic Services (O.S.S.) during World War II. But already Donovan was making a name for himself in this war.

The young poet-sergeant was in the intelligence section and could have remained at regimental headquarters, but he preferred work as a combat scout alongside "Wild Bill" Donovan. Donovan in turn regarded his young sergeant highly as a military scout and observer.

Late in July the Rainbow Division centered its attack on the heights overlooking the Ourcq River valley. The Allied leaders knew that once these heights were taken the Germans could not possibly keep their hold on the Ourcq River.

The fighting at the Ourcq River was some of the most bitter of the war. On July 28 the village of Sergy was taken and retaken several times until the Rainbow men finally held it. Losses were severe.

Two days later the Rainbow continued its advance. Major Donovan led a scouting party to look over the situation ahead and to locate and silence enemy machine guns. Although he was not told to do so, his young sergeant followed Donovan. The patrol was moving through a forest with machine-gun and small-arms fire raking the forest pathways.

Once again the Rainbow men used their Indian tactics of moving forward on their stomachs a few painful yards at a time. It was slow, hard, nerve-racking work.

After a time Major Donovan looked around for his sergeant. He was nowhere to be found. Donovan then began to search for him in earnest. A few moments later he found the sergeant lying on his stomach and peering over a small rise as though he were observing the enemy out in front of him. But his eyes would see no more. Sergeant Joyce Kilmer, author of the poem "Trees," was dead, a bullet through his brain.

After the war Kilmer and many of his brave comrades who also fell during this battle were buried at the American Oise-Aisne cemetery in France. The following inscription was made on the cemetery chapel:

THESE ENDURED ALL AND GAVE ALL
THAT HONOR AND JUSTICE MIGHT
PREVAIL AND THAT THE WORLD MIGHT
ENJOY FREEDOM AND INHERIT PEACE

American units proved their worth in fighting elsewhere on the Western Front as the Allies went over to the offensive. On August 8 the British attacked in the

Somme area. The United States 33rd and 80th Divisions took part in this offensive. The British used several hundred tanks to break through the mass entanglements of barbed wire in No Man's Land, taking the startled Germans completely by surprise, overrunning their positions and taking thousands of prisoners. After the war General Erich von Ludendorff described the opening day of this offensive as "the black day of the German army in the World War."

With the general retreat by the Germans in August, the bombardment of Paris by Big Bertha came to an end. This brought rejoicing throughout the city. Everyone still wondered, of course, just what kind of a monster gun could have shelled them from such a distance. For this answer they would have to wait until the end of the war. Then it would be learned that Big Bertha was not one gun but several developed for the Krupps by a Dr. von Eberhardt.

Big Bertha's site was the forest of Coucy near Laon. Here there were three of the long-range guns, each weighing more than 150 tons. If stood on end, each gun would have been as tall as a ten-story building. The gun carriage itself was 25 feet high. The base on which the gun carriage revolved had ball bearings as large as bowling balls. The artillery shells fired by the guns weighed about 250 pounds. In flight the shells reached a height of 25 miles. So great was the distance each shell had to travel that the curvature and rotation of the earth had to be carefully considered in aiming and firing the gun.

There were several of these guns because each one could only fire a comparatively few times—perhaps 50 or 60—before its barrel was worn out and had to be rebored. The people of Paris would no doubt have been pleased to know that at least one of the guns exploded while it was being fired, killing most of its 17-man crew.

But none of this could they know until the war ended. And before that happy day much hard fighting lay ahead —both on land and in the air.

Eight

*Land And
Air Victory
At
St. Mihiel*

American divisions had fought so well in every battle in which they had been used so far in the war that General Pershing now felt a separate American army should be formed. General Foch apparently agreed. The American First Army became official on August 10, 1918. Its headquarters were at Neufchateau on the Meuse River south of St. Mihiel.

At St. Mihiel the Germans had held a salient jutting deep into the Allied lines ever since 1914. The first task of the newly formed American First Army was to drive the enemy from this salient. This would make possible a further attack on key German railroad and supply centers at Metz and Sedan. It would also free Allied lateral rail and supply lines for an offensive all along the Western Front.

The St. Mihiel offensive was scheduled to begin in mid-September. Just before it took place, however, General Foch had a change of heart. He decided the First Army should be broken up and some of its divisions used elsewhere on the Western Front.

Pershing refused to allow this. He told Foch that the First Army could, of course, be used anywhere Foch as Allied Commander-in-Chief saw fit to use it, but now that it was formed it could not be broken up once more into separate divisions. After much argument Foch agreed to abide by Pershing's wishes. Pershing on his part agreed to use fewer troops than he had originally planned on using in the St. Mihiel attack. He also agreed to start making immediate preparations for a major attack in the Meuse River-Argonne Forest region. The men held out of the St. Mihiel drive would be used to start the Meuse-Argonne attack, but plans were also made to use some divisions in both campaigns.

This gave the American First Army an almost impossible task. It meant that Pershing had to launch two major offensives within a period of from two to three weeks on fronts some 40 miles apart. Such a feat had never before been performed in World War I.

The St. Mihiel Campaign began on September 12 and ended with overwhelming success on September 16. More than half a million Americans from the following ten divisions were involved: 1st, 2nd, 4th, 5th, 26th, 42nd, 78th, 82nd, 89th, and 90th. They suffered about 7,000 casualties but captured 16,000 prisoners. About 100,000 French troops also took part. When the offensive ended the Germans had been driven completely out of the salient. The American Tank Corps under General S. D. Rockenbach had its first experience in combat during this campaign. It aided greatly in the quick reduction of the salient.

In direct support of this major American infantry and armored corps drive was an Allied air force that played a key role in the victory at St. Mihiel. This was the largest single air campaign of the war, and in it the fledgling American Air Service came of age. American flyers piloted more than 600 of the 1,500 French and British aircraft that took part in the offensive. More than 400 of these planes were bombers, the bombers Billy Mitchell had included in his original plans for the A.E.F. Air Service. Now Mitchell was seeing those plans fulfilled. What was more, he was able to direct this air campaign himself.

Both Billy Mitchell and the A.E.F. Air Service had come a long way since that day in Paris the year before when Mitchell and Pershing had talked together for the first time. After that meeting Pershing had made General William Kenly, an artillery officer, Chief of the Air Service. Later he had appointed General Benjamin Foulois to replace Kenly. Foulois had been in turn succeeded by Pershing's old West Point classmate, General Mason Patrick. These three men were able leaders, but none seemed to be exactly the person needed to make the American Air Service a first-rate fighting command. Billy Mitchell had continued to fly and fight the enemy daily, and his name was on everyone's lips as the man who should have the job. Even General Foulois had told Pershing that Mitchell actually should be the Chief of the Air Service instead of himself.

Pershing finally bowed to the inevitable. In August

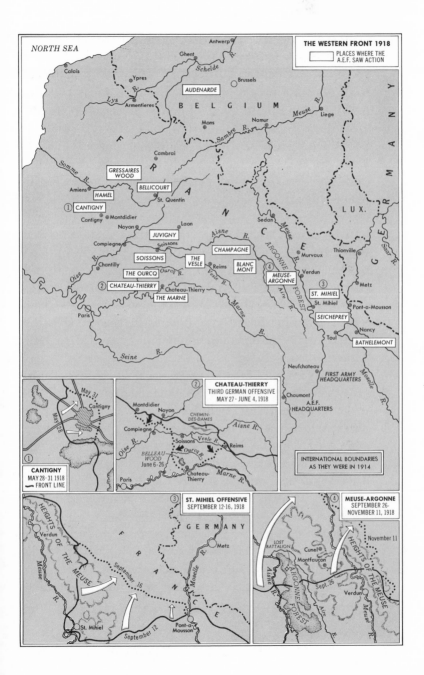

THE WESTERN FRONT 1918
☐ PLACES WHERE THE A.E.F. SAW ACTION

NORTH SEA

BELGIUM

Antwerp
Ghent
Schelde R.
Brussels
AUDENARDE
Calais
Ypres
Lys R.
Armentieres
Mons
Namur
Meuse R.
Liege
LUX.
GERMANY

F R A N C E

Cambrai
Somme R.
GRESSAIRES WOOD
BELLICOURT
Amiens
HAMEL
St. Quentin
① CANTIGNY
Cantigny
Montdidier
Noyon
Laon
Sedan
Murvaux
Thionville
Saar R.
Metz
Pont-a-Mousson

JUVIGNY
Soissons
Aisne R.
ARGONNE FOREST
Compiegne
SOISSONS
THE VESLE
CHAMPAGNE
Reims
BLANC MONT
④ MEUSE-ARGONNE
Verdun
③ ST. MIHIEL
St. Mihiel
Oise R.
Chantilly
THE OURCQ
Ourcq R.
② CHATEAU-THIERRY
Chateau-Thierry
Vesle R.
THE MARNE
SEICHEPREY
Nancy
Toul
BATHELEMONT

Paris
Marne R.
Seine R.
Neufchateau
FIRST ARMY HEADQUARTERS
Chaumont
A.E.F. HEADQUARTERS
Moselle R.

CANTIGNY
MAY 28-31 1918
— FRONT LINE
May 31
Cantigny
May 28

② CHATEAU-THIERRY
THIRD GERMAN OFFENSIVE
MAY 27 - JUNE 4, 1918
Montdidier
Noyon
CHEMIN-DES-DAMES
Aisne R.
Compiegne
Oise R.
Vesle R.
Soissons
Ourcq R.
Reims
BELLEAU WOOD
June 6-26
Paris
Chateau-Thierry
Marne R.

INTERNATIONAL BOUNDARIES
AS THEY WERE IN 1914

③ ST. MIHIEL OFFENSIVE
SEPTEMBER 12-16, 1918
GERMANY
HEIGHTS OF THE MEUSE
Verdun
Meuse R.
F R A N C E
Metz
Moselle R.
September 16
St. Mihiel
September 12
Pont-a-Mousson

④ MEUSE-ARGONNE
SEPTEMBER 26-
NOVEMBER 11, 1918
November 11
LOST BATTALION
Cunel
Montfaucon
ARGONNE FOREST
Aire R.
Aisne R.
Sept. 26
HEIGHTS OF THE MEUSE
Verdun
Meuse R.

1918, a few weeks before the St. Mihiel campaign was to begin, Colonel William Mitchell was named Chief of the Air Service, First Army. Colonel Mitchell—who would shortly be Brigadier General Mitchell—now had a chance to fulfill his dreams of becoming the war's outstanding air combat commander.

Eddie Rickenbacker had also come into his own. A pursuit pilot now, he was already an Ace and was on his way to becoming America's Ace of Aces—the flyer who would shoot down more enemy planes than any other American.

Eddie Rickenbacker was the kind of war hero that Americans on both the home front and fighting front took to their hearts. He was a young man who had come up the hard way, but he had learned something with each step along that difficult path.

Born in Columbus, Ohio, in 1890, he was one of seven children whose father died when Eddie was twelve years of age.

The day after Eddie's father was buried, the youngster went to work in a local factory, earning $3.50 a week. He worked the night shift, walking to and from the factory to save carfare. At the end of each week he turned over his entire pay to his mother. This love for his mother was to give Eddie Rickenbacker strength all of his life, even when he grew up and became America's top fighter pilot. On one of his most difficult days in the air war against Germany, the fabric ripped from one of the wings of his Nieuport pursuit ship, and it looked as if he were going to crash and be killed. He thought of what a tragic blow the news of his death would be to his mother, and the picture of her grief gave him the renewed courage and determination that enabled him to bring his battered plane back across the Allied lines.

As a boy still in his teens young Eddie became interested in motors, and he took correspondence courses in engineering and drafting. When he was 20 he took up automobile racing and was soon winning championships in the United States and abroad. He was in England when America entered World War I. He had hurried home eager to suggest his plan for a squadron of flyers composed of racing-car drivers. When that plan had been turned down, Rickenbacker had gladly accepted General Pershing's offer to accompany him to France—mainly because he wanted to be near the front. As Pershing had anticipated, Rickenbacker had not been in France very long before he asked for a transfer to the Air Service.

He was sent to Tours in France for his first flight training in August 1917. His natural mechanical ability plus a supreme desire to become a combat flyer made it possible for Rickenbacker to take his first solo flight after only 12 trips with an instructor. After only a few more hours of training (in World War II a fighter pilot had several hundred hours of flight training before he was sent into combat) Rickenbacker was transferred to the 94th Aero Pursuit Squadron.

The planes of the 94th bore a red-white-and-blue insignia. This design included an Uncle Sam stovepipe hat with stars and stripes on its crown. The hat was encircled by a ring, giving the unit its nickname: the Hat-in-the-Ring squadron. It was to become the most famous of all the American pursuit squadrons.

The Hat-in-the-Ring squadron was the first American-trained air unit to go into action against the enemy. It served longer in combat than any other air service squadron. It was credited with shooting down the first and last German airplanes shot down by the American Air Service. It shot down 69 planes, more than any other American squadron. It had the first official American Ace, Lieutenant Douglas Campbell, as well as the greatest American Ace, Captain Eddie Rickenbacker.

When Rickenbacker reported for duty with the Hat-in-the-Ring squadron, it was commanded by Major Raoul Lufbery, a veteran flyer who had shot down 17 planes while flying with the Lafayette Escadrille before America entered the war. Lufbery was one of several hundred American volunteers who had been flying with the French and British since the start of the war. The Lafayette Escadrille was the most famous of these volunteer units.

About 65 Americans also flew as pilots on the Italian Front. One of these pilots was Captain Fiorello LaGuardia, who many years later became the Mayor of New York City.

The Lafayette Escadrille had been formed as an American unit within the French Flying Corps in 1916. At first it was called the American Escadrille, but the German State Department protested that an American flying unit in combat was a violation of United States neutrality. Shortly afterwards the organization's name was changed to the Lafayette Escadrille in honor of the Marquis de Lafayette.

Many of the men of the Lafayette Escadrille became famous while shooting down 199 German planes. Lufbery was not merely famous because of his individual combat record. He was also highly regarded as a leader. As commander of the Escadrille he worked out a number of aerial tactics to use against Germany's leading Ace, Baron Manfred von Richthofen, and his Flying Circus. Richthofen's red-nosed Fokkers were the scourge of the air over the Western Front, particularly when they adopted mass formation flying against the Allied airmen.

Against these mass attacks Lufbery had his men form their planes into a circle in the air with each plane protecting the plane in front. When the men of the Lafayette Escadrille were flying two-place ships with an observer in the rear, the observer could pick off any German plane that tried to enter this circle. This maneuver was based on the method American pioneers used in drawing their covered wagons into a circle in protection against the Indians. This "Lufbery Show" or "Lufbery Circle" was used by all air forces in fighter-plane combat right up through the Korean War.

In February 1918 the Lafayette Escadrille became the 103rd Pursuit Squadron in the American Air Service. Lufbery was made commander of the 103rd's sister squadron, the 94th. Tragically, Lufbery was to lose his life on May 19 when his plane was set afire in combat. He had always advised his men never to jump if their planes caught fire, because there was always the chance of their being able to land safely. If they jumped, he pointed out, they would have no chance at all. When his plane went up in flames, however, Lufbery leaped out and was killed. Because there was a small stream near where Lufbery fell some of his friends thought he might have been trying to save himself by leaping into it.

Lufbery, as well as a number of other Allied airmen, probably would have survived if parachutes had been available. For some reason, however, parachutes were never worn by Allied airplane pilots. During the last six months of the war many German pilots parachuted to safety, but American, French, and British flyers never had this opportunity. Balloon observers also had parachutes which they used just as soon as their balloons were attacked.

Before his death Major Lufbery was able to take Eddie Rickenbacker and Douglas Campbell on their first flight over the German lines. Lufbery's careful instruction and the watchful way in which he shepherded his inexperienced flyers in their first flights were lessons Rickenbacker never forgot. When he himself was placed in command of the Hat-in-the-Ring squadron in September 1918, Rickenbacker was like a watchful father over his untried young flyers. Not only did he lead them on their first patrols as Lufbery had done, but on more than one occasion Rickenbacker credited them with victories that he could truly have claimed for himself. Rickenbacker finally was credited with 26 victories, but every member of his command agreed that he shot down at least a dozen other planes for which he received no credit.

Rickenbacker's sense of fair play went even further. Today, when chivalry in warfare seems perhaps dead, a line from the diary of America's greatest air hero of World War I still has a gallant ring. On March 10, 1918, Rickenbacker wrote: "I will never shoot a Hun who is at a disadvantage, regardless of what he would do in such a position."

Rickenbacker's personal code in leading his own men into battle was also a noble one. He never asked one of his pilots to fly a combat patrol he himself would not fly. In addition he made it a point of honor never to let a member of his squadron fly more hours against the enemy than their leader. More than once Rickenbacker went on

America's Ace-of-Aces in World War I, Captain Eddie Rickenbacker, standing in front of his Spad plane on the Western Front. (U.S. Signal Corps photograph in the National Archives).

voluntary patrols when the day's regular patrols had been flown just to make certain he was taking his equal share of risk.

The Hat-in-the-Ring squadron first flew into combat from Toul in April 1918. On April 14 Lieutenant Alan Winslow and Lieutenant Douglas Campbell shot down the squadron's first planes. Within a month Rickenbacker was an Ace.

During their first weeks in combat the 94th flew French Nieuports. These were not the best planes in the air, by any means. There were no American planes available, however, and the American squadrons had to do the best they could with the planes they received from the Allies. Later the Hat-in-the-Ring squadron, as well as the 95th Aero Pursuit Squadron with whom the 94th shared an airfield, flew French Spads. The Spad was more of a match for the German Fokker, although the Fokker could fly higher and dive more swiftly than the Spad. The best of the British ships at this period of the war was the Sopwith Camel. During the entire war Camel pilots shot down more than 1,600 aircraft, more than fighter pilots flying any other type of plane have ever shot down.

In May the American Air Service had four squadrons at the front—the 27th, 94th, 95th, and 147th. These squadrons were formed into the 1st Pursuit Group. In July the 1st Pursuit Group played a key role during the Second Battle of the Marne as they fought the famed Richthofen Flying Circus to a standstill. It was during this fighting that young Quentin Roosevelt was killed.

Baron von Richthofen was now dead, and his Circus was commanded by a Captain Wilhelm Reinhardt. Later the Richthofen Circus was led by Hermann Goering, who scored 22 victories in World War I. This was the same Goering who would one day become the head of Germany's *Luftwaffe* during World War II. During the month they faced each other in daily combat during the Second Battle of the Marne, the 1st Pursuit Group suffered 36 pilot casualties and the Richthofen Circus had 38 men shot down.

The record of victories of the American Air Service grew as its pilots learned new lessons in daily combat against the enemy. Eddie Rickenbacker was an especially determined student. He was not a wild, reckless flyer, nor a lone wolf. He was a team flyer in every sense of the word. Although brave and daring, he did not believe in flying into battle in a blind rage and thus putting himself at a disadvantage against a more coldly calculating enemy. Just as he had done all of his life up to now, he set out to learn the "why" and "how" of his job. It was a matter of life and death that he do so. Aerial warfare was a grim, unforgiving business. Few pilots survived even one mistake. Evidence of this was the fact that during the course of the war the 94th Pursuit squadron suffered a 100 per cent turnover in flying personnel because of dead or wounded pilots.

Rickenbacker soon learned that a successful pursuit pilot had to know the limitations of his own aircraft. If the wings on a Nieuport buckled in pulling out of a fast dive, then it was up to the wise Nieuport pilot not to try and outdive a Fokker. If a Spad had certain other limitations against a Fokker, then it was up to the Spad pilot to recognize those limitations. Another observation he was forced into making was that all too often when he had an enemy in his gunsights, his guns would suddenly jam. He decided that irregularities in some shell casings caused the jamming. To avoid this he personally inspected every shell that was placed in the machine-gun belts of his aerial guns. He instructed the men who flew with him to do likewise.

Slowly but surely these knowledgeable actions began to pay off and Rickenbacker's personal victory tally began to mount. He was awarded a number of French and American decorations, including the highest award given its military men by the United States: the Congressional Medal of Honor. He received the Medal of Honor for fearlessly attacking seven enemy planes and shooting down two of them while he was flying a voluntary patrol.

As a team flyer, however, Rickenbacker was not satisfied with only his personal achievement. He wanted his team, the Hat-in-the-Ring squadron, to lead all other American squadrons. When he assumed command of the 94th, the 27th squadron had a larger total number of victories. Rickenbacker told all of the Hat-in-the-Ring mechanics that he wanted every pursuit ship in the squadron ready for flight duty every day. He told his pilots that he expected the 94th to gain the lead in victories within a few days and never lose it. Rather than spur his men on by getting them to compete among themselves, he urged the 94th to compete as a team against all of the other squadrons of the American Air Service.

Rickenbacker assumed command of the 94th squadron on September 15 at the peak of the St. Mihiel offensive. On his first day in combat after being named the Hat-in-the-Ring squadron commander Rickenbacker shot down two German planes just to fulfill his part of the challenge he had just given his men. Fired by the follow-me spirit of their leader, the flyers of the 94th Hat-in-the-Ring squadron soon took over the lead in aerial victories and held it until the end of the war.

*   *   *

Not all flyers, however, were able to adopt Rickenbacker's wise, sane, team-play approach to aerial combat. There were others who flew with reckless gallantry into battle and scored spectacular victories day-after-incredible-day—men who lived alone, fought alone, and all too frequently died alone. It was because of the feats of one such man that the 27th Aero Squadron temporarily led the 94th Aero Squadron in total victories. This heroic lone wolf was Frank Luke, the balloon buster from Arizona.

*   *   *

During a period beginning on September 12, the first day of the St. Mihiel campaign, and ending just 17 days later, Frank Luke shot down 18 or 19 enemy balloons and airplanes. This was more aircraft than any other member of the American Air Service had shot down at this time. His career as a pursuit pilot ended with his death in a church graveyard at Murvaux, France, on September 29. He died at the age of 21.

Born at Phoenix, Arizona, in 1897, Frank Luke was one of nine children. Their father was a German immigrant. Young Frank went to work in a local copper mine after graduating from high school. He was silent as an Indian and had few friends. When America went to war, one of

Frank's brothers enlisted in the Army and his sister Eva became a Red Cross nurse. It was Eva who talked Frank into joining the Signal Corps. He wasn't interested in the infantry because he disliked discipline of any kind, but he thought that as a member of the Signal Corps he could get to be a pursuit pilot and continue to lead an independent life of action.

After preliminary flight training in the United States Frank was commissioned a second lieutenant on January 23, 1918. He was then sent to France, where he took advanced flight training at Issoudun, learning to fly Nieuports and Spads. He was assigned to the 27th Aero Pursuit Squadron of the 1st Pursuit Group near Château-Thierry in late July 1918. Later the squadron was moved to Rembercourt near Verdun.

On one of his very first flights over the enemy lines Frank was carefully instructed by his squadron commander to stay in formation. Luke decided, however, to go Hun-hunting on his own. When asked afterward why he had dropped out of formation, Luke said he had engine trouble. A day or two later he returned from one of these lone-wolf flights insisting he had shot down a German Fokker, but no one would believe him. After that he carried a pad of paper and a pencil with him. Whenever he shot down a German plane or balloon he landed at the nearest Allied position and got front-line observers to confirm his claim.

His flying companion—Luke continued to have few friends—came to be Lieutenant Joseph Wehner. Wehner's ancestry, like Luke's, was German, and Luke felt this gave them a common bond.

Luke had not flown in combat long before he became

Lieutenant Frank Luke, the famed "balloon-buster from Arizona," just 10 days before his death in a combat action that earned him the Congressional Medal of Honor. (U.S. Signal Corps photograph in the National Archives).

interested in the possibility of shooting down enemy observation balloons. Most Allied fighter pilots shied away from attacking German balloons because they were heavily defended by anti-aircraft guns as well as by several squadrons of fighter planes. This, plus the fact that it was rumored that each German balloon cost about $100,000, was a challenge that Luke could not resist.

On September 12 Luke went into action and shot down his first *Drachen,* as the German balloons were called. A few days later he shot down several more. By this time he and Wehner had worked out a system for Luke's attacks. While the Arizona balloon buster was roaring into attack the balloons, Wehner flew nearby to protect him from German Fokkers. The two pursuit pilots also discovered that the best time to attack the balloons was right at dusk when the *Drachen* were being lowered to the ground.

On September 16 Luke and Wehner collaborated to shoot down another trio of balloons. Word had been going up and down the front about the 27th Aero Squadron's mounting victories, and Colonel Billy Mitchell was on hand to watch Luke and Wehner put on their show on this evening. He saw each one of the three balloons go up in flames, and when Luke and Wehner returned to the field Mitchell counted over 100 bullet holes in the two men's airplanes. Their ships were repaired by the following day, however, and they went out and scored additional victories.

On September 18 Luke put on what was perhaps his greatest show when he bagged two more balloons, two Fokkers, and an observation plane. To set one of the balloons on fire, he had to fly within 50 feet of the ground. Finishing off the second balloon, he saw that Joe Wehner was in trouble, and he dived into a squadron of Fokkers, shooting down two of them. He then high-tailed it for home but managed to bag an observation ship before reaching his field. His tally was now three or four planes (the records vary) and ten balloons, giving him 13 or 14 victories to Eddie Rickenbacker's nine. But this proved to be a joyless day for Luke. Joe Wehner failed to return from this mission.

Luke had never spoken more than a few single-syllable words to his fellow flyers. Now he refused to talk to anyone, and he seemed to think of nothing but getting back into combat. Bad weather, however, prevented him from taking to the air until September 26. That day he shot down a Fokker, and the next day he bagged a balloon. To knock down this balloon, he had to come down to within 25 or 30 feet of the ground and fly through a flaming wall of defensive fire.

On September 29, his last day in the air, Luke spotted three enemy balloons near Verdun. Following his custom of making certain that he got credit for his victories, Luke dropped a message to some Allied front-line observers telling them to keep their eyes on the trio of *Drachen*. Within a matter of minutes he had set the first one aflame. On this attack, however, he was jumped by nine or ten Fokkers and was badly wounded.

Ignoring the wound and the fact that his Spad was also seriously damaged, he roared in to knock down the second balloon. The Fokkers kept after him, causing further damage to his ship. As he flew in to get the third balloon, he was faced with an inferno of anti-aircraft fire, but he flew unwaveringly through it and scored his final victory. In an apparent effort to avoid the Fokkers who lay in wait for him, Luke took evasive action and headed toward the Meuse River flying at treetop level.

As he approached the village of Murvaux he saw that its streets were filled with German troops. He machine-gunned them before his plane was forced down in the local church graveyard. As soon as he landed, Luke whipped out his automatic and managed to struggle from his plane. In a few moments he was completely surrounded by German infantry who demanded that he surrender. Luke's response was to empty his automatic at them. The Germans opened up with point-blank rifle fire, and moments later the balloon buster from Arizona lay dead.

For conspicuous gallantry on his last flight, Lieutenant Frank Luke was posthumously awarded the Congressional Medal of Honor. Many years later Luke Air Force Base in Arizona was named for him.

*   *   *

St. Mihiel was the first battle of the war in which United States infantry and flyers fought as a completely independent Army and Air Service under an American Commander-in-Chief. The victory gave a tremendous boost to Allied morale and was a crushing blow to the Germans.

Marshal Foch described the American First Army and Air Service as "magnificent" at St. Mihiel. He also told French officers to visit the First Army front to learn how the American infantry had made its way so quickly through what had been thought of as "impassable" German barbed wire entanglements, defensive trenches, and other obstacles. General Pershing's early demands for an army

When the United States First Army went into action in the autumn of 1918, the Yanks lived up to the predictions of their Commander, General Pershing, that they could break through the German defenses. (U.S. Army photograph).

trained to fight independently using an open style of warfare were now paying off.

Pershing now turned his attention to the far more difficult Meuse-Argonne offensive.

Nine

*The
Lost Battalion
In The
Meuse-Argonne
Campaign*

The Meuse-Argonne campaign was so called because to the right or east of the attacking First Army lay the Meuse River, and to its left or west lay the Argonne Forest. (The doughboys called it the "Oregon Forest".) This was an exceedingly difficult area to attack. Pershing had chosen it because he believed only American soldiers who had been trained especially for this type of warfare were capable of taking the German defense positions by frontal assault.

Along the Meuse there were high, wooded hills controlled by the Germans. From these heights of the Meuse the enemy could catch the Americans in a crossfire (called *enfilading* fire) as they advanced up the valley. The Argonne Forest was also hilly and densely wooded, a perfect cover for machine-gun nests.

The machine gun and rapid fire artillery accounted for more than three-quarters of the casualties on the Western Front. These Yanks are shown in the Argonne Forest, where a single team of machine gunners could hold off hundreds of the enemy. (U.S. Signal Corps photograph in the National Archives).

Across this region between the Meuse River and the Argonne Forest the Germans had built defensive positions a dozen miles deep. Barbed wire, machine-gun nests, and concrete artillery emplacements made these positions impregnable—or so the Germans thought. They also had built deep lines of permanent trenches and strongpoints from which they believed they could fight off any attack.

At the center of the area between the Meuse River and the Argonne Forest was the strongly fortified hill of Montfaucon. This was a key defensive stronghold. Marshal Foch's prediction was that Montfaucon might not be captured until 1919.

Mounting a second major offensive in the Meuse-Argonne region while the St. Mihiel attack was still going on was an enormously difficult feat. The person mainly responsible for its success was Colonel George C. Marshall, assistant chief of staff for operations in the First Army. In World War II Marshall became Chief of Staff of the entire United States Army, and after that war he was Secretary of State under President Harry S. Truman.

In order to get the Meuse-Argonne offensive under way, Marshall had to move more than half-a-million Americans into the Argonne sector from St. Mihiel in two weeks time. Equipment and several thousand heavy guns also had to be transferred. All this was done at night so that the enemy would be unaware that an attack was being mounted.

The doughboys who took part in this gigantic troop movement experienced a nightmare of automobiles, trucks, motorcycles, horses, mules, artillery caissons, supply wagons, tanks, and endless lines of other men moving through the black night. In the pitch dark everything seemed to be in a hopeless snarl. And there was the added discomfort of the endless rain beating down on "tin hats" that fitted poorly and gave a man a pounding headache, and the heavy hob-nailed boots that weighed four pounds each and worked blisters on a soldier's feet.

The endless columns of equipment and men would move forward fifty feet and halt, move forward ten feet and halt, move forward twenty-five feet and halt. Exhausted men sometimes lay down in the mud beside the road and slept. Sometimes when they awakened they were hopelessly lost from their units.

Yet somehow order was brought out of all this confusion and the Meuse-Argonne offensive was begun as scheduled.

The attack began on the morning of September 26. Four of the nine American divisions that took part in the first part of the assault had had no previous combat experience. The more experienced divisions were still at St. Mihiel. Nevertheless these untried troops captured Montfaucon on the second day of the attack. They continued to make slow, steady progress until October 3, when their advance was stopped by the enemy.

Bad weather was a serious problem for both the infantry and flyers. First Army veterans always remembered the heavy rains and the deep mud that were part of the Argonne fighting—and they remembered correctly. According to official records rain fell in the area on every day except seven between September 26 and November 11.

As at St. Mihiel, aircraft and tanks played important roles. After the first few days of fighting, however, the First Army suffered seriously from a shortage of tanks to break through the enemy's defenses. Before this shortage occurred one of the tank brigades that was extremely suc-

A British invention, the tank was used by the Americans to overcome the German defense positions at St. Mihiel and in the Meuse-Argonne campaign. (U.S. Signal Corps photograph in the National Archives).

cessful was led by a fiery colonel, George S. Patton, Jr. Patton was wounded and won the Distinguished Service Cross early in the Argonne attack. The Germans would remember "Old Blood 'n Guts" Patton again in World War II when his Third Army started from St. Lô in Normandy and went slashing across France in one of the greatest advances in military history.

Pershing now replaced green troops with more experienced divisions, and on October 4 the attack once more rolled forward. The Germans now began throwing their best divisions into the defense. They also began calling upon their reserves from elsewhere on the Western Front. This slowed down the American advance in the Argonne, but it aided the attacks that were being made by the British, French, and Belgian armies farther north. In this fighting outside the Argonne three American divisions, the 27th, 30th, and 37th, served with the British and French at Cambrai, Le Catelet, and St. Quentin.

In the Argonne Forest itself the Germans put up a desperate resistance. The Americans were having to fight for the forest a tree at a time, and individual deeds of heroism were being performed hourly. It was here between October 2 and October 7 that the famed "Lost Battalion" made its legendary stand.

*　　*　　*

"Sergeant."

"What?"

"I just heard some voices back there."

"So what?"

In attacking machine gun nests the Yankee doughboys adopted Indian style tactics, crawling forward on their stomachs and digging in every few yards. This picture was taken in the face of heavy rifle and machine gun fire in the Meuse-Argonne fighting. (U.S. Signal Corps photograph in the National Archives).

"They were talking German."

"Back where?"

The soldier pointed.

"You're crazy," the sergeant said. "We just came from back there. The Boche are up front."

"The Boche may be up front, but they're *behind* us too, because I heard some voices behind us—a lot of them —and they were talking German."

A star shell suddenly lit the night. By its light the sergeant carefully studied the soldier's serious face. "O.K.," the sergeant said finally. "I'll tell the Major about it."

It took the sergeant some little time to find Major Charles Whittlesey, the battalion commander.

"Yes, Sergeant, what is it?" Major Whittlesey asked.

"Sir, one of my men thinks he heard some Germans to our rear."

"He's imagining things—or dreaming," Major Whittlesey said. "Tell him to get some sleep. You'd better do the same thing, Sergeant. We've got a rough day ahead of us tomorrow."

"Yes, sir."

But when the battalion sergeant major had left, Major Whittlesey felt more than a little uneasy. He certainly hoped he and his men hadn't advanced so rapidly today that they had lost contact with the rest of the 77th Division.

Major Whittlesey was in charge of a mixed battalion of about 550 men that included six companies from the 308th Infantry Regiment, one company from the 307th Infantry Regiment, and two companies from the 306th Machine Gun Battalion. This morning, October 2, Whittlesey had been given orders by General Robert Alexander to advance as rapidly as he could through the Argonne Forest without worrying about keeping in contact with units to the left, right, or rear.

"The orders," General Alexander had added, "are direct from General Pershing, and they say we're to take the Argonne Forest by frontal assault if necessary no matter what our casualties are."

Major Whittlesey's mixed battalion had jumped off at dawn. Their destination was the Charlevaux Valley. They had advanced slowly but steadily all day. And all day Whittlesey had worried about the lack of contact with other units. There had been some opposition but not the kind of opposition they were used to. This had made Whittlesey even more uneasy. Were the Germans leading them into a trap?

By nightfall they had reached Charlevaux Brook and dug in on the far slope. Now, with the men bedded down for the night, Major Whittlesey lay sleepless, thinking about what the battalion sergeant major had just told him. Was it possible that the battalion was cut off and surrounded by the enemy?

The next morning, however, Major Whittlesey felt somewhat more optimistic after talking things over with Captain George McMurtry, his second in command. Whittlesey also sent a message to Captain Nelson Holderman, who was in command of the company from the 307th Infantry that had dug in on the right flank. When he received a reply from Holderman, Whittlesey felt further confidence in the situation.

By now the Germans had begun shelling the Americans with artillery. Machine-gun fire also raked the position, and shells from the *Minenwerfer* (German trench mortars) were causing a number of casualties. Most of the Americans had dug deep foxholes, but these were not much protection against mortars.

Whittlesey now sent a runner with a message back to headquarters asking for artillery support. When the runner did not return and no Allied heavy guns were heard, the Major sent back another runner with a message —and another, and still another. None got through. Word soon arrived at Whittlesey's command post that all of the messengers had been killed by the Germans.

And then the major got the news he had been dreading: the Germans *had* worked their way in behind the Americans. They had strung up barbed wire and set up machine guns. The American battalion was cut off.

Major Whittlesey now quickly wrote another note calling for artillery support. This one was written on very thin tissue paper. It would have to be sent to headquarters by carrier pigeon, their only means of communication now that their runner posts had been broken.

Major Whittlesey asked one of his men how many carrier pigeons they had.

"Just seven, sir."

Whittlesey inserted his message in a capsule that was clipped to the pigeon's leg, and the bird was released. If the winged messenger weren't shot down, the message should soon arrive at the 77th Division's pigeon loft. From there it would be rushed to headquarters.

It apparently took the Germans until noon on October 3 to realize that a mixed battalion of Americans was

Lieutenant Colonel Charles Whittlesey, Commander of the Lost Battalion. (U.S. Army photograph).

trapped and surrounded on one slope of the Charlevaux Valley near the old Charlevaux mill. As soon as they realized this, the Germans increased the volume of their trench mortar fire and artillery bombardment. Evidently they felt there was no need for an infantry assault on the American battalion's position. It could be taken by siege.

Major Whittlesey gave no thought to retreat—to fighting his way through the Germans at his battalion's rear and re-establishing contact with the rest of the 77th Division. Before the attack General Alexander had issued blunt orders stating that any ground that was once taken could not be given up without direct written orders from him. And First Army Commander General Pershing had made his feelings equally clear. "Any captured position," he said, "should be held at all costs."

Major Whittlesey knew that a battle seldom went the way it was planned, and it was very important for a commander not to be too upset by this fact. In a way a plan for a battle was like a football play. On a blackboard with every player carrying out his assignment, every football play looked perfect. But it seldom worked out that way. If it did, every play would score a touchdown. Under actual game conditions things were always different. Signals were misunderstood. Key blocks were missed. A defensive player moved into a different spot on the field from where the play on the blackboard had shown he would be.

And so it was in battle. Once the guns started firing and the advance got under way all sorts of confusing elements entered the picture. Communications broke down. Certain defensive positions proved stronger in reality than they had looked on the battle map. Some men were braver than others. Military men even had a name for this confusion that was always present under combat conditions. They called it the "fog of battle" or the "fog of war."

The inexperienced leader might panic when he suddenly realized that he didn't know exactly what was going on around him. The experienced military leader, Major Whittlesey knew, expected to encounter this confusion and was not upset by it. The all-important thing in a situation such as the one in which they now found themselves was to keep their heads and hold the ground they had captured. To panic now would be to invite defeat. Major Whittlesey determined to hold his ground until division headquarters could act to relieve them.

"Here we are and here we stay," he said now to Captain McMurtry. He also told the captain to issue orders for every man in the battalion to hold his ground to the last round of ammunition and then prepare to defend their position in hand-to-hand combat if necessary.

Whittlesey had no mistaken idea about how easy it was going to be to hold their position. His spirit of fierce determination, however, quickly communicated itself to all of his men. It had not always been so.

Tall, long-legged, and near-sighted, Major Whittlesey had been the butt of many jokes when the 77th Division was in training at Camp Upton, New York. "Old bird legs," they called him. Since those training days, however, the men of the 308th battalion had come to respect this quiet New Englander who never asked them to take a risk that he would not take himself. A lawyer in civilian life, he was not much given to talk in the front lines, where actions spoke louder than courtroom words.

He now made a tour of inspection of their position,

despite the shells falling around him. He told his men to get set for a tough afternoon and night.

"They'll be up here to relieve us in the morning," he reassured them.

"How come we're not getting any artillery support?" one of the men asked.

Before the Major could answer another soldier cut in, "Because they don't know where we are. We're lost out here."

"They know where we are all right," Major Whittlesey said firmly. "It's just a matter of time until they get to us. I'm sure headquarters has had word from us by now. I've sent out several more messages by carrier pigeon."

But the men felt certain none had got through. They had even seen some of the pigeons shot down.

The next day there was still no relief in sight. The men waited with the dogged determination of battle-tried infantrymen. Then, in a sudden rush, there was a German infantry assault on Captain Holderman's position.

Holderman had been wounded early in the siege. Despite this fact he had continued to encourage the other officers and men in his company. On their second day under attack Holderman was again wounded, but he continued to lead his men. At one point he risked direct machine-gun fire as he crawled into the open to rescue several soldiers who had been wounded. Now, with the Germans attempting a frontal assault on the battalion's right flank, Holderman rallied his men, and they beat off the attackers.

Major Whittlesey tried sending several more messages

by carrier pigeon, but the alert German riflemen spotted the birds in flight and shot them down.

Now, however, something far worse than the Major or any of his command had feared began to happen. Once again shells began to fall on their position, but these were not German shells. They were coming from behind, from the Allied artillery positions. They were being bombarded by their own guns!

Desperately Major Whittlesey called for the battalion's last carrier pigeon. This brave little bird *must* get through to headquarters with a message asking the Allied artillerymen to lift their barrage.

This last carrier pigeon was named *Cher Ami* (Dear Friend). It was one of 600 birds that had been donated by pigeon fanciers in Great Britain to be trained by the Americans to carry messages. The United States Army had first experimented with pigeons for military use as early as 1878 when it bought some birds and sent them to the 5th Infantry Regiment in the Dakota Territory. Large numbers of hawks in the area preyed on the birds, however, and use of them was dropped for a time. Ten years later the Army established a loft at Key West, Florida, and resumed its carrier pigeon experiments.

Some pigeons had been sent with General Pershing's troops on the punitive expedition to Mexico. By the time America entered World War I pigeons had more than proved their worth as messengers, and the Army had some 20,000 of them. There were about 5,000 of the birds on combat duty in France. *Cher Ami* was to prove the most heroic of all the combat birds.

Whittlesey wrote his message hurriedly and it was inserted in the capsule on *Cher Ami's* leg. Then the bird was released. It had flown only a short way, however, before the men saw it seemingly stop in mid-flight and then plummet downward. Their last hope seemed dead. But then, miraculously, the brave bird struggled back into flight and headed toward the Allied lines.

Cher Ami proved to be a dear friend indeed. Thirty minutes after he had left Charlevaux Valley he landed at the 77th Division's pigeon loft at Rampont some 25 miles away. One leg had been shattered by a bullet, one wing was badly injured, and his breastbone was broken by shell fire. But the message was there, dangling from the shattered leg.

A short time later the barrage was stopped.

Another message had also arrived at 77th Division headquarters. This was from General Pershing directing that every effort be made to get relief to the beleaguered men of what everyone in France was now calling the "Lost Battalion."

Efforts were, of course, being made to do just that, but now these efforts were redoubled. No one, however, seemed able to exactly locate the position of Whittlesey and his men.

Meanwhile, the Lost Battalion continued to stand off German shellfire and infantry attacks. The besieged men were now without food and water. They had eaten their iron rations during the first two days, and attempts to get to Charlevaux Brook for canteens of water had ended in the men who tried to do so getting shot.

Attempts to get food and other supplies to the Lost Battalion included numerous flights by the 50th Aero Squadron. Most of the food and medical supplies they dropped, however, fell into German hands or just out of

CHER AMI, *the carrier pigeon that proved a "dear friend" of the Lost Battalion. (Smithsonian Institution).*

reach of the Americans. Despite the fact that several planes were shot down by the Germans, the rescue flights continued. On October 6 Lieutenant Harold E. Goettler and Lieutenant Erwin R. Bleckley flew down the Charlevaux valley just a few yards above the ground in a determined effort to pinpoint the position of the Lost Battalion for an accurate supply drop. Both pilots were killed. After the war they were awarded the Congressional Medal of Honor for their heroic action.

Without letup the Germans continued to shell the Lost Battalion's position and to rake it with rifle and machine-gun fire. Major Whittlesey continued to ignore the murderous attack as he walked among his men giving them reassurance and encouragement. Captain McMurtry was equally brave, despite the fact that he was wounded once by shrapnel and again by a hand grenade.

Encouragement was badly needed, especially when the Germans brought a new weapon to bear on the men on the embattled hillside. This was the dreaded *flammenwerfer* (flame thrower), which most of the men had never seen before. The badly wounded Captain Holderman led his men in an attack against this fearful weapon, killing the Germans wielding it.

For several days now the men of the Lost Battalion had been living on tree leaves and roots. Desperate for something nourishing to eat, a few of the men tried to crawl out and get the food packages that had been dropped by the 50th Aero Squadron. As a result several of the men were shot and others captured by the Germans.

One of the men who was captured was Private Lowell Hollingshead. Shortly after his capture he was surprised to find himself talking with a German lieutenant who spoke excellent English. This was Lieutenant Heinrich Prinz, a German intelligence officer who had lived in Seattle, Washington, for some years before the war. Prinz tried his best to get Hollingshead to give him information of military value, but Hollingshead gave him only his name, rank, and serial number. Then Prinz told Hollingshead he wanted him to return to the Lost Battalion with a note demanding that Major Whittlesey and his remaining men surrender. At first Hollingshead also refused to do this, believing that anything he did at the request of the Germans would be an act of disloyalty to his buddies. Finally, however, he was blindfolded, given the surrender demand and sent carrying a white flag back to the Lost Battalion. The letter he delivered to Major Whittlesey contained a missing date, several misspellings and other mistakes. It read:

To The Commanding Officer of the 2nd Batl.J.308
of the 77th American Division.

Sir.

The Bearer of the present, Lowell R. Hollingshead, has been taken prisoner by us on October _____ He refused to the German Intelligence Officer every answer to his questiones and is quite an honourable fellow, doing honour to his fatherland in the strictest sense of the word.

He has been charged against his will, believing in doing wrong to his country, in carrying forward this present letter to the Officer in charge of the 2nd Batl.J.R.308 of

the 77th Div. with the purpose to recommend this Com-
mander to surrender with his forces as it would be quite
useless to resist any more in view of the present conditions.

The suffering of your wounded man can be heared over
here in the German lines and we are appealing to your
human sentiments.

A withe Flag shown by one of your man will tell us that
you agree with these conditions.

Please treat the Lowell R. Hollingshead as an honour-
able man. He is quite asoldier we envy you.

The German commanding officer.

Meanwhile, Major Whittlesey had asked for a volunteer
to try to carry a message to division headquarters and then
lead a relief party to the Lost Battalion. Despite the fact
that every runner who had tried to make his way through
the Germans at the rear of the Lost Battalion had been
killed, Private Abraham Krotoshinsky volunteered for the
dangerous mission.

Krotoshinsky set out at dawn on the morning of October
7. He was weak with hunger and battle fatigue, but he
was determined to get through the German lines. He
crouched and ran part of the way and crawled when he hit
an open space. Once when he lay in hiding beneath some
bushes a German officer walked past and stepped on
Krotoshinsky's hand. He almost bit through his lip to
keep from crying out. He lay there for several hours before coming out of hiding. Then he started to run and
crawl again, thinking of nothing but the importance of
getting through with the message.

That evening Krotoshinsky stumbled into what he

To The Commanding Officer of the 2nd Batl.J.R.308

of the 77th American Division.

Sir.

The Bearer of the present, Lowell R Hollingshead
has been taken prisoner by us on October
He refused to the German intelligence Officer every answer to his questiones and is quite an honourable fellow, doing honour to his fatherland in the strictest sense of the word.

He has been charged against his will, believing in doing wrong
to his country, in carrying forward this present letter to the Officer
in charge of the 2nd Batl.J.R.308 of the 77th Div. with the purpose to
recommend this Commander to surrender with his forces as it would be
quite useless to resist any more in wiew of the present conditions.

The suffering of your wounded man can be he heared over here
in the German lines and we are appealing to your human sentiments.

A withe Flag shown by one of your man will tell us that you
agree with these conditions.

Please treat the Lowell R Hollingshead as an honourable man.
He is quite a soldier we envy you.

The German commanding officer.

*This is a photostatic copy of the actual surrender demand sent to
the Commander of the Lost Battalion by the Germans. The docu-
ment is mounted under glass in the library at Williams College, Lieutenant Colonel Whittlesey's alma mater. (Williams College Library).*

thought was an abandoned trench. Then he heard voices, American voices. Now he was afraid that he might be shot because he did not know the password that this American unit would be using. Nevertheless he shouted that he was an American, and finally several infantry scouts came forward. They took him to headquarters where Krotoshinsky gave the commanding officer the exact location of the Lost Battalion.

After a quick meal, the weary but happy Krotoshinsky volunteered to return with the relief party. That night, October 7, the Lost Battalion was relieved by hard-driving infantry units fighting their way through the Germans. For his heroic efforts Krotoshinsky was awarded the Distinguished Service Cross.

When the Lost Battalion was relieved, Major Whittlesey was again besieged—this time by newspaper men who had been sending stories all over the world about the gallant stand of the Lost Battalion from the first day it had been surrounded. The reporters, when they heard about the German surrender note, flashed a story to their papers saying that Major Whittlesey had replied to the Germans by telling them to go to blazes. Actually, as Whittlesey kept insisting, he had not replied to the note at all. He said he felt it did not deserve a reply. This was his way of being completely scornful of the Germans' demand. But the legend of Whittlesey's "Go to blazes!" remark grew, and few people wanted to hear him deny that he had made it.

Whittlesey was personally thanked for his heroic stand by General Pershing. He was also promoted to lieutenant colonel and awarded the Congressional Medal of Honor. Captain McMurtry was promoted to major, and he and

Captain Holderman were also awarded the Medal of Honor.

Of the approximately 550 men who had gone into the Argonne Forest and been trapped in Charlevaux Valley, 107 were killed and only 194 were able to walk out when their relief arrived. Most of these 194 brave men immediately volunteered to go forward with other elements of the 77th Division and finish the fighting.

And what of *Cher Ami*, the "dear friend" of the Lost Battalion?

Cher Ami was not forgotten. In fact General Pershing personally saw to it that the wounded bird hero was awarded a special medal for gallantry. Pershing also gave orders for the bird to be returned to the United States in the officers' cabin of the army transport *Ohioan*. In America *Cher Ami* received the best of medical care in an effort to prolong his life, but he lived only until the year after the war, 1919. When *Cher Ami* died, he was stuffed and mounted and placed on exhibition at the Smithsonian Institution in Washington, D. C.

In the days that followed the relief of the Lost Battalion, the American drive to clear the Argonne Forest continued relentlessly. During this fighting there were many more individuals who performed deeds of bravery above and beyond the call of duty. Two men, however, were almost unbelievably heroic. The first was Corporal (later Sergeant) Alvin C. York, and the second was Lieutenant (later Captain) Samuel Woodfill.

General Pershing called York the outstanding civilian

soldier of World War I, and Marshal Foch described York's feat as the most remarkable piece of heroism performed by any soldier in the fighting on the Western Front. Pershing said Woodfill was the greatest of all the American heroes of the war.

Ten

*The
Civilian-Soldier
And
The Regular
Army Man*

"Well, Corporal," Brigadier General Lindsay said, "I understand we don't have to do any more fighting."

"How's that, sir?" the corporal asked.

General Lindsay grinned. "Because your company commander tells me you just captured the whole blasted Hun army."

Corporal Alvin York looked uncomfortable. "I guess it wasn't quite the *whole* army, sir. Just a hundred and thirty-two of 'em."

"Just a hundred and thirty-two!"

"Yes, sir."

The General exploded with laughter. "Single-handed?" he managed to ask.

"More or less, sir."

General Lindsay shook his head with amazement.

Men all along the Western Front were equally amazed when they learned about York's feat. They just could not believe that one man could capture that many German infantrymen—and crack Prussian Guards at that. But the story was true, every word of it.

Corporal Alvin York—who later became world-famous as Sergeant York—was a mountain man from Fentress County, Tennessee. He had not wanted to join the Army. He had, in fact, been a conscientious objector because of his religious beliefs. His pastor, however, as well as his first commanding officer in the Army had persuaded him that it was his moral duty to serve his country in this war. Once convinced that America and the Allies were fighting for the right, York became a soldier—and a great one.

York was a member of the 82nd Division. Men from Georgia, Alabama, and Tennessee were the backbone of this hard-fighting outfit, but a number of its members also came from many of the other states of the Union. For this reason the 82nd was often called the All-American Division.

Corporal York's heroic deed in the Argonne was performed on October 8, the day after the Lost Battalion was relieved. On this day York and 15 other men of the 82nd Division's 328th Infantry Regiment were led by Sergeant Bernard Early in an attack on a German machine-gun battalion.

By crawling forward Indian fashion the 16 men managed to work their way to the rear of the machine-gun nests. They then rushed one of the positions, capturing several officers and men. Other Germans only 40 or 50 yards away saw this action and turned their guns on the

Sergeant Alvin C. York, whom General Pershing called "The outstanding civilian soldier of World War I." (U.S. Army photograph).

Americans. Before the Germans fired, however, they called to their comrades who had been taken prisoner, telling them to fall to the ground. Then the German machine gunners raked the American infantrymen, killing six of them and wounding three. Sergeant Early was one of the men who was wounded.

York now took command. He placed the German prisoners in the hands of the unwounded Americans. Then he worked out a plan to defeat the remaining Germans single-handed. His plan was based on his many years of experience in turkey-shooting contests back in Tennessee. In a turkey shoot a bird would be tied behind a log so that only its head could bob up occasionally. The marksman had to shoot and hit the turkey's head in the brief instant it was visible above the log. York now brought his ability as a turkey-shooting marksman into play. In order to try and draw a bead on York the Germans had to raise their heads above the sandbags that protected their machine-gun nests. Whenever a German raised his head, York picked him off.

After York had killed about a dozen of the Germans, a Prussian officer and half a dozen men charged him. Once again the Tennessee mountain man called upon his experience as a hunter. Rather than shoot the German nearest to him, York first picked off the last man, then the next-to-last and so on. Afterwards he explained that this was how wild turkeys were shot, so that the ones in front didn't know the ones in back were being hit. In this fashion York dropped all of the onrushing attackers before any of them knew what was happening to the others.

The German major in charge of the Prussian Guard machine-gun battalion now offered to surrender his command of about 90 men—if York would please just stop shooting. York signalled the Germans to come forward with their hands in the air. As they filed toward him, York saw that one of the Germans was carrying a half-concealed hand grenade. York shot him, and the rest of the prisoners fell meekly into line. York placed the major in front of him and told the other Americans to bring up the rear with the remaining prisoners.

The German major tried to point out the path they should follow, but York led his party in the opposite direction. He knew the major was trying to lead him into a trap.

As they moved toward the American lines they encountered more and more German machine-gun nests. With York prodding him in the back with his service revolver, the major urged his fellow soldiers to cry, "Kamerad!," which was the word the Germans used when they wanted to surrender.

York disarmed these new prisoners and added them to his bag for the day. Finally they reached the American lines, and he reported to his company commander, Lieutenant Ralph Woods, telling him he had a few Germans to turn over to him.

"How many are there, Corporal?" Lieutenant Woods asked.

"I kind of lost track, sir."

In addition to the 132 prisoners he had captured, the Tennessee corporal who had never wanted to be a soldier had killed some 20 Germans and silenced about 40 machine guns.

*   *   *

Samuel Woodfill was a Regular Army man who loved being a spit-and-polish soldier. Before World War I he had served at a hundred bleak Army outposts, drilled on count-less dusty parade grounds, and faithfully stood guard-mount in the dim watches of many a lonely night. In the Philippines and on the Mexican border he had an out-standing record as a sergeant. When the war started he was temporarily promoted to the rank of lieutenant. Later he became a captain.

Woodfill's one fear had been that he might not get to France in time to take part in the fighting. However, his division arrived in France on May 1, 1918, and Woodfill and his comrades-in-arms were soon in the thick of the battle.

Woodfill was a member of the 5th Division, and the Germans had come to fear the men who wore its Red Diamond insignia. At St. Mihiel and in the early stages of the Meuse-Argonne offensive, the Red Diamond rifle-men fired so rapidly and accurately that the Germans thought—as they thought when they faced the Rainbow Division—that the men of the 5th were all armed with machine guns. "They kill anything that moves," the Germans said.

On October 12, four days after Corporal York's feat, Lieutenant Woodfill was leading his company from the 60th Infantry Regiment in an attack near the village of Cunel. Like Montfaucon, Cunel occupied high ground and was heavily fortified. It was an ideal defensive position.

Suddenly the advance of Woodfill and his men was stopped by heavy machine-gun fire. Woodfill waved his men to take cover, and he proceeded to advance alone. Inching forward on his stomach, he managed to work his way around to the rear of one of the machine-gun nests. He had crawled to within a few yards of the position when he and the Germans saw each other at the same time.

Samuel Woodfill, described by General Pershing as "The greatest of all the American heroes of the war." Woodfill became a captain during the war, but reverted to his regular army rank of sergeant after the Armistice. (U.S. Signal Corps photograph in the National Archives).

There were four Germans, and all of them started to fire at Woodfill.

In a division of expert marksmen Woodfill was among the best. He had spent hundreds of hours on the rifle and pistol ranges during his long service as a peacetime soldier. But that was shooting at stationary targets. Now he was having his first try at targets that moved and shot back. Woodfill was able to drop three of the Germans with his rifle, but the fourth made a diving tackle at him and wrestled him to the ground. Woodfill was finally able to free his service pistol and shoot the German.

Woodfill now waved his company forward.

They had gone only a few yards, however, when another machine gun opened up, spewing death. Once again Woodfill dashed forward alone and, shooting from the hip, knocked out this second nest. Several more Germans were killed in this attack. Woodfill also took several others prisoner, turning them over to the men of his company.

Again Woodfill pumped his arm up and down rapidly. This was the traditional infantry signal for his company to move forward at the double. The men had scarcely started to advance when a third machine gun began to chatter in front of them. Once more the gallant lieutenant waved his men to a halt, while he charged ahead alone. When he reached the machine gun he saw there were five Germans manning it. He killed them with the last five shells in his rifle. Just as he was about to jump into the machine-gun pit, however, two other Germans a few yards away turned their machine gun on him. Firing his pistol again, Woodfill managed to get the Germans to duck back behind their sandbags, but he failed to hit them. Out of ammunition now, Woodfill saw a pick handle lying on the ground. He seized this, rushed the two Germans and was able to overcome them before they could shoot him.

When Woodfill signalled his company forward this final time, his men were so inspired by their lieutenant's bravery that they swept all opposition before them.

*   *   *

In mid-October the United States Second Army was formed at Toul. Major General Robert Bullard was placed in command of its forces near St. Mihiel, while Lieutenant General Hunter Liggett was named to take over Pershing's post as commander of the First Army. Pershing now was the group commander in charge of two American armies along a more than 100-mile front. This was about one-quarter of the length of the entire Western Front.

On November 1 the third and final phase of the Meuse-Argonne campaign began with assaults by the First Army on the last line of the German defense system, the Hindenburg Line. The advance went swiftly forward until the heights above Sedan were captured. This broke the Germans' main rail-supply line. On November 6 the German high command requested terms for an armistice. On November 7 Germany's Kaiser Wilhelm abdicated and fled to the Netherlands, where he was to live in exile for more than 20 years. On November 11, 1918, an armistice was signed at Compiègne, and World War I was ended.

In summing up the results of the Meuse-Argonne campaign, General Pershing said: "Between September 26 and November 11, 22 American and 4 French divisions, on the front extending from southeast of Verdun to the Argonne Forest, engaged and decisively defeated 46 dif-

141

ferent German divisions, representing 25 per cent of the enemy's entire division strength on the Western Front. The First Army suffered a loss of about 117,000 killed and wounded. It captured 26,000 prisoners, 847 cannon, 3,000 machine guns, and large quantities of material."

The following divisions took part in the Meuse-Argonne campaign: 1st, 2nd, 3rd, 4th, 6th, 26th, 28th, 29th, 32nd, 33rd, 35th, 36th, 42nd, 77th, 78th, 80th, 81st, 82nd, 89th, 90th, 91st, and 92nd.

More than 1,200,000 Americans had taken part in the 47 days of fighting in the Meuse-Argonne offensive. It was the greatest battle in American history until World War II.

The fighting ended almost a year to the day after the A.E.F. suffered its first casualties in the trenches at Bathelemont. Since that day it had met the enemy on a dozen fields of battle and had lost to him on none.

First there had been the successful attack at Cantigny. This had been followed by the Second Battle of the Marne: the defense of Paris near Château-Thierry, the counterattack against Soissons, and the drive that forced the Germans back across the Vesle River. The reduction of the St. Mihiel salient had been completed with swift success. And finally the Meuse-Argonne campaign had ended brilliantly after a month and a half of the most desperate kind of fighting. The American fighting man's raw courage had been tested in the fires of the Western Front; and, as had always been true in the past, it had not been found wanting.

Most of the doughboys on the Western Front accepted victory quietly. One of them said afterwards: "We were too cold and wet and worn out to do much celebrating. The end of the fighting really came as a kind of anticlimax.

142

We'd been hearing rumors of an Armistice for so long that when it actually came we couldn't believe it. In fact we'd even had a kind of joke about the Armistice. It wasn't very funny maybe—just a simple kind of soldier's joke.

"When the fighting in the Argonne was at its worst we kept hearing stories about President Wilson's famous 'Fourteen Points' on which the Armistice should be based. We also heard the Kaiser would only accept ten of the points. One of our sergeants said, 'Let's get Wilson and Kaiser Bill up here in the front lines and maybe they'll compromise on six points.'

"Anyway, on the afternoon of November 11 our outfit was told that an Armistice had been in effect since eleven o'clock that morning. There were a few half-hearted cheers, but that was about all. I guess we really didn't believe it until that night when a few of the boys began to gather firewood and build fires. That brought the end of the war home to us—the fact that you could build fires and sit by them and get warm and dry right out in the open. Then we looked around us and all along the Western Front we saw the lights from other fires, and we began to believe that maybe it was true, the fighting had really stopped."

*　　　*　　　*

The cost of World War I in both lives and money was staggering. No completely accurate figures have ever been compiled, but it has been estimated that there were more than 30,000,000 men killed and wounded among all of the warring nations. Allied losses were more than 5,000,000 killed and died and almost 13,000,000 wounded. The Central Powers' losses were more than 3,000,000 killed and died and more than 8,000,000 wounded. The United States suffered 53,407 deaths and had 204,002 men wounded.

The direct cost of the war in money amounted to about 300 billion dollars. (Indirect costs are incalculable.) If this money had been made into silver dollars and stacked along the Western Front, it would have made a wall more than 400 miles long, twenty-four inches thick, and seven feet high.

The United States spent about $2,000,000 an hour from April 6, 1917, to November 11, 1918. Its total expenditure, not including loans to the Allies, was 22 billion dollars. This total meant that during World War I the United States spent as much money as it did for all of its government costs from 1791 to 1914.

Eleven

The
Unknown
Soldier

On November 11, 1921, an unidentified soldier of the United States of America who had died in World War I was buried in Arlington National Cemetery across the Potomac River from Washington, D. C.

The Congress of the United States had approved this ceremony by a public resolution on March 4, 1921. One unidentified body was then taken from each of four American cemeteries in France. They were placed in identical caskets and carried by truck to the city hall at Châlons-sur-Marne. Inside the city hall the caskets were placed side-by-side and draped with American flags.

Sergeant Edward F. Younger of the headquarters company, 2nd Battalion, 50th United States Infantry, was chosen to select the body for return to the United States as the Unknown Soldier. Younger was from Chicago, Ill.

145

An orphan, he had joined the regular army at 18. He had gone overseas with the 9th United States Infantry in September 1917. He fought at Château-Thierry and in the St. Mihiel campaign and was wounded twice. Many years later he himself would be buried at Arlington.

On October 24, 1921, Sergeant Younger entered the room in the city hall containing the caskets. He was carrying a bouquet of roses given him by M. Brasseur Brulfur, a Frenchman who had lost two sons during the war. Sergeant Younger slowly walked around the caskets, pausing in solemn and reverent thought before each one. After some minutes he placed the bouquet of roses on the second casket. Then he came to attention and saluted smartly.

Later that day the casket was carried to the local railroad station. Boy Scouts carrying flowers marched in this procession. At the railroad station the French band played *The Star-Spangled Banner*, while the Unknown Soldier was placed in a special funeral car in a train furnished for the occasion by the French government.

The United States cruiser *Olympia,* carrying the Unknown Soldier, sailed from Le Havre on October 25 and arrived at the Navy Yard in Washington, D. C., on November 9. The casket was then placed on an artillery caisson and taken to the rotunda of the United States Capitol. There it rested on the same bier that had held the remains of Presidents Abraham Lincoln, James Garfield, and William McKinley.

On Armistice Day (now Veterans' Day), the casket was taken on its last journey to Arlington National Cemetery. Riding in a carriage behind the Unknown Soldier was ex-President Woodrow Wilson, who had led the nation through the trials of World War I. Wilson was now gravely ill and would die in 1924.

One of the pallbearers was Samuel Woodfill, legendary

Medal of Honor winner of the Meuse-Argonne campaign. Woodfill had remained in the Army after the war, reverting in grade to sergeant. There were also many other war heroes present as honorary pallbearers at the Arlington ceremonies. Lieutenant Colonel Charles Whittlesey, commander of the Lost Battalion, was there, as was his second in command, Major George McMurtry. Medal of Honor winners Captain Nelson Holderman and Sergeant Alvin York were also there, but America's Ace of Aces, Captain Eddie Rickenbacker was not.

Rickenbacker had been invited to the ceremonies, of course, and planned to attend. But the renowned racing car driver and pursuit pilot who had driven through countless difficult situations during his racing career and had piloted his way through swarms of enemy planes now found himself caught hopelessly in a Washington traffic jam. Thus he and several other dignitaries were forced to miss the ceremonies.

There were many other heroes, sung and unsung, who could not attend. These were the brave men who had died in Europe during the war. It was they whom the Unknown Soldier represented—the men of America who gave their lives to defend their country.

They were also represented, however, by one who was living, the man who had seen the A.E.F. grow from a handful of green rookie troops to victorious millions—General John J. Pershing. Although he had been decorated many times, the only decoration Pershing wore on this day was the one every A.E.F. veteran could wear—the Victory Medal. Pershing stood beside President and Mrs. Warren Harding and Vice President and Mrs. Calvin Coolidge as the Unknown Soldier was laid to rest at Arlington and "Taps" was played over the grave.

The casket of the Unknown Soldier was placed on two

inches of soil brought from the battlefields of France. This soil was placed within the steel vault that held the casket. Ten years later the tomb was completed over the grave. It is a solid block of marble weighing about 50 tons. On one side of the tomb was carved the following inscription:

HERE RESTS IN

HONORED GLORY

AN AMERICAN

SOLDIER

KNOWN BUT TO GOD

Today this tomb is called "The Tomb of the Unknowns." The remains of unidentified soldiers from both World War II and the Korean War were buried on either side of the Unknown Soldier of World War I on Memorial Day, May 30, 1958. A constant vigil is kept by an Army honor guard. At rigid attention this honor guard walks the post of the Unknown Soldier twenty-four hours a day, 365 days a year, in all kinds of weather.

And not far from the Tomb of the Unknowns the body of General John J. Pershing lies buried. There is no hero's monument over his grave. Before his death in 1948, Pershing requested that he be buried among his men at Arlington and that no monument be erected to him. Instead the marker over the Commander of the A.E.F.'s grave is a small, simple stone no larger than that over the graves of many of the men in the ranks of the American Expeditionary Forces who lie buried nearby.

Books
About
World War I

The Air Force Blue Book (Bobbs-Merrill, 1960).

American Battle Monuments Commission. *American Armies and Battlefields in Europe* (Government Printing Office, 1938).

The Army Almanac (Stackpole Company, 1959).

The Army Blue Book (Bobbs-Merrill, 1960).

Boatner, Mark M., III. *Army Lore* (Pacific Stars and Stripes, 1954).

Cameron, James. *1914* (Rinehart, 1959).

Compton's Pictured Encyclopedia (F. E. Compton). Article on World War I and related biographies.

Cowan, Samuel K. *Sergeant York and His People* (Funk & Wagnalls, 1922).

Duffy, Francis P. *Father Duffy's Story* (Doran, 1919).

Dupuy, Richard E. *The Compact History of the United States Army* (Hawthorn Books, 1956).

Esposito, Vincent J. *The West Point Atlas of American Wars: vol. 2 1900-1953* (Praeger, 1959).

Goldberg, Alfred, ed. *A History of the United States Air Force* (Van Nostrand, 1957).

Gurney, Gene. *Five Down and Glory: A History of the American Air Ace* (Putnam, 1958).

Hoehling, Adolph A. and Mary. *The Last Voyage of the Lusitania* (Holt, 1956).

Holliday, Robert C., ed. Joyce Kilmer: *Poems, Essays and Letters* (Doran, 1918).

Jacobs, Bruce. *Heroes of the Army: the Medal of Honor and Its Winners* (Norton, 1956).

Johnson, Thomas M. and Pratt, Fletcher. *The Lost Battalion* (Bobbs-Merrill, 1938).

McCollum, L. C. *History and Rhymes of the Lost Battalion* (The Author, 1929).

Miller, Henry W. *The Paris Gun* (Jonathan Cape & Harrison Smith, 1930).

Millis, Walter. *Arms and Men* (Putnam, 1956).

The Navy Blue Book (Bobbs-Merrill, 1960).

Pershing, John J. *Final Report* (Government Printing Office, 1919).

Pershing, John J. *My Experiences in the World War, 2 vols.* (Stokes, 1931).

Potter, E. B., ed. *The United States and World Sea Power* (Prentice-Hall, 1955).

Reynolds, Quentin. *They Fought for the Sky* (Rinehart, 1957).

Rickenbacker, Edward V. *Fighting the Flying Circus* (Stokes, 1919).

Seymour, Charles. *Woodrow Wilson and the World War: vol. 23, pt. 2 Chronicles of America* (Yale University Press, 1921).

Slosson, Preston W. *The Great Crusade and After: 1914-1928* (Macmillan, 1930).

Thomason, John W. *Fix Bayonets!* (Scribner, 1926).

Tompkins, Raymond S. *The Story of the Rainbow Division* (Boni & Liveright, 1919).

Tuchman, Barbara W. *The Guns of August* (Macmillan, 1962).

Van Every, Dale. *The A.E.F. in Battle* (Appleton, 1928).

Whitehouse, A. G. J. *The Years of the Sky Kings* (Doubleday, 1959).

Wolff, Leon. *In Flanders Fields: the 1917 Campaign* (Viking, 1958).

Wood, William and Gabriel, Ralph H. *In Defense of Liberty: vol. 7 The Pageant of America* (Yale University Press, 1928).

York, Alvin C. *Sergeant York: His Own Life Story and War Diary* (Doubleday, 1928).

Index

153

21 Oct 99